M000223683

Published by Arrangement with J. C. Phelps

First Printing, October, 2009 (10)


NEWPUB Books are published by
Phelps Publishing
16202 Spring Valley Road, Piedmont, South Dakota, 57769

For:
Alexandra
Edy
Jim
Rick
Robert
&
Robert

Special thanks to:
Bobbe
Lynn
Guy Richard

# Chapter One

I lay quietly in the wet grass with one eye closed and the other gazing through the sight of my .50 cal. sniper rifle. I'd been watching the compound for six days and was aching for some action. Waiting has never been conducive to improving my focus. With my active imagination, I usually found my mind wandering. However, over the past couple of months I'd learned how to daydream and pay attention at the same time.

White and Blue had been pushing sniper training down my throat. I couldn't remember the last time I'd sat in front of my T.V. or my computer. My fingers itched to poke at the keys on my keyboard.

I'd graduated college with a degree in computer science and only realized my mistake after I'd spent several months as a data processor. But, as I lay in the tall, wet grass, trying not to shiver, I gave a quiet sigh of mourning for my decision to drop my first career choice. My regrets didn't last long as I tried to mentally put myself back into my former cubical. At least out here I had some variety. I could be cold, wet, hungry or all three at the same time. That, at least, put some adventure into my life.

Getting over my longing for my old life in record time, my mind continued to wander. My eyes still captured everything around me but my main thoughts centered on the day I was assigned this job.

White had called me down to the office and I hoped it was for a new job assignment. I was becoming restless with all the sniper training. It seemed to consist mostly of laying around outside, eluding detection monitoring the area.

For some reason I never envisioned myself on a real sniping mission. The thought of actually killing someone with my coveted rifle had been happily absent throughout my months of training for just that. I had killed a man once and it was terribly unpleasant. I found myself pushing that thought out of my head more often than was healthy.

"I'll never forget my first kill," I whispered to myself as I returned my full attention back to the compound. *My first kill*, I thought to myself with a sick feeling in my stomach. Why did I have to think of it that way? My first kill... like I was going to become a mass murderer or something. With the words "mass murderer" my mind started to meander down a new path. Masked murderer came to mind and then I thought of my mother.

Less than six months ago, White and I had discovered the identity of the famed sniper, known only as Penumbra. My mother.

My whole life I'd thought of my mother as just that, my mother. I had no idea she led another life. And not just any other life but a life full of death. Death she caused.

Before we found out, no one but my father knew the identity of Penumbra and many theories floated around. Some thought he was a Russian, some thought he was many people taking the name of Penumbra after a job but, as far as I knew, almost all of them thought he was a *he*. My mother's true identity came as a shock to me but explained a lot about my own life. I'd looked at her differently for about a month but then I realized my mother was my mother, no matter what.

White looked at *me* differently after our discovery. He obviously assumed it was in my blood to be a killer but I couldn't disagree more. The last thing I wanted to do was to run around the world killing bad guys.

So why was I out here? My thoughts turned back to the day White called me down to the office.

I'd only gotten home from a training mission the night before so the early morning call was a bit of a surprise. Hoping for a real job, I dressed quickly and rode the elevator down to the seventh floor office.

Gabriella, the company secretary, wasn't in her usual seat yet but all of my partners were in White's office. White spoke up, using Ms. Grey instead of Alex for the first time in months.

All partners were given "company" names. White's real name is Rick Malone and mine is Alexis Stanton. Before joining White and Associates I introduced myself as Alex but I didn't have much contact with people outside the company any more and the name Ms. Grey was used more often than not. I will admit I've grown quite fond of my new name.

"Ms. Grey, we have a job for you." White's tone was semi enthusiastic as he handed me my briefing envelope.

I made myself more comfortable in my chair and pulled out satellite pictures of a compound and a picture of a man and his dossier. It listed personal information such as his age, height and weight and he had a curious marking on his left hand. His name, however, was not on the page. This seemed unusual to me, but I let it slide.

"We don't think you'll have to enter the compound, but you and Green can go through the security system before you leave, just in case." White added.

Mr. Green, known to family and friends as Seth Caldwell, is our company security specialist. He'd be the one to talk to if you needed to get into a place, unnoticed.

"What am I doing?" I looked back to the paperwork to find my objective.

"We need this man eliminated." Red spoke up. He seemed to be judging my reaction as he told me this so I made sure to show no emotion. Red is an alias for Aidan Tierney and I like to think of him as the company's shrink, but his title is Communications Specialist. He's a licensed psychiatrist and fluent in many different languages. I don't know if he treats the men extensively on the psychiatry level, but I do know he's always in charge of the interrogations the company performs.

"Black and I have been assigned as your chauffeurs." Brown rolled his eyes in a mock complaint. Mr. Brown, AKA Josh Braun, was an averagely built man with an unceasing smile and a playful personality.

I had grown to like him immensely after I laid down the ground rules. He thought he could chide me about being the only woman in the company and what my true role might be, with thick insinuation toward a sexual aspect. I didn't take kindly to those kinds of jokes and I made it very clear.

Brown's expertise lies with the company vehicles. He's an astounding mechanic and driving/flight instructor. He'd been giving me flight instructions before our most recent job, now referred to as the K&G job, and again afterwards. I was by no means an expert pilot, but I knew enough that I could go up alone and actually return safely to the ground.

Blue had walked to the closet while Brown grumbled and came back with my sniper rifle, still in the case. I'd been using it regularly but when he handed it to me this time my stomach flipped and my mouth went dry.

"I made a few modifications last night and the ammo you will be using is inside the case." Blues given name is Shane Lochlann and he's the company doctor/sniper. I've always thought it was a strange combination and when I asked him about it, he said he just fell into it. He'd always wanted to be a doctor but the Navy pushed him into the sniper role because he was such a good marksman.

"What kind of modifications?" I asked.

"I've added a laser sight. It's a neat one. It only lights up when you start to pull the trigger. You won't be giving your position away unless you sit with your finger on the trigger."

When we were all satisfied with the briefing Black said, "Let's go," nodding his head toward the door. He most certainly was a man of few words but when he had something to say, everyone listened. His was the first name that was given to me freely by any of the men.

Adam Quinn, AKA Mr. Black, is a huge man with a shaved head, a deep voice and a tendency toward chivalry. He has always tried to look out for me, within reason. And what I mean by 'within reason' is if I were wrong, Black would be the first to point it out. He knows I am a hard worker and won't stop until I either have it right or there is no question that I can't get any better. The other men in the company didn't always know that of me and started out a little aloof.

Black, Brown and I boarded the chopper and several hours later they dropped me off with nothing but a couple of memorized GPS locations, some water and a small amount of dried food. I hiked my way through dense forest and located the compound in a couple of hours. I thanked the powers that be for the darkness that still surrounded me. Several times during my hike I pictured killing the target but pushed it as deep as I could, as fast as I could.

I crawled from the woods and hid myself in the grass. There I awaited the sun. I stayed in one position for the entire first day and that night I scouted around a little more. By sunrise on the third day I could recite the entire routine in the compound. The man I was sent to permanently remove had yet to make an appearance. Late night of the fifth day, three vehicles were let into the compound and I got a glimpse of my target. He was obviously a prisoner with his hands cuffed in front of him. They had his head covered with some kind of sack and I only identified him with the mark on his hand. I wasn't satisfied with my identification without being able to see his face, so I hesitated and then I couldn't get a clear shot. They led him to a heavily guarded building and he remained there all night.

Although I wasn't happy with this mission, my fear of failure was driving me forward. That's why I was here. I didn't want to disappoint my partners. I'd missed my opportunity last night and hoped it wouldn't be my only one.

I started to warm up as the sun rose. The compound bustled with activity before the sun was very high and I didn't miss anything. The sun hadn't lit the sky for more than an hour when a chopper set down inside the compound. Within minutes, the door to the building opened and I saw the man once more. I couldn't get a clean shot and only managed short glimpses of the prisoner but they had put some sort of sensors all over his head and face. One of the escorts held the door open while another put what looked like a pillow case over the mans head. I made a double check on the prisoner by moving my sights to his left hand. The mark was there and I was satisfied he was the target. I waited for them to start leading him to the chopper so I would have a clean shot. Before I was ready, the man I had studied a week ago was in my sights and now all I had to do was pull the trigger. The convoy of guards and the prisoner had exited the building a few seconds earlier and were walking toward a chopper that was obviously going to fly him off somewhere and I would lose my chance. It was either shoot now or I could wait to see if he ever came back. My stomach churned but I pulled the trigger and felt the kick of the weapon. I closed my eyes, but only for the length of a blink. I didn't want to watch this, but I had to make sure my target was down.

Everything slowed in my mind and the moment when he should fall came too soon. I was an excellent marksman and I knew the timing was wrong. The only people that noticed anything had happened were those directly near the target and they didn't seem too surprised. Then the sound of the gunshot must have finally reached the compound. Through my scope I noticed people ducking and scurrying this way and that and I felt a little better. The men that had been walking near the target had surrounded him so I wasn't able to see if he was dead and I didn't dare leave until I knew but I had to get out of there. Then a small gap between the men let me see enough to believe I had accomplished my mission. I realized I was grateful for the pillowcase because it shielded me from the full truth. I remained where I was for about two seconds more and was rewarded with solid confirmation. One of the men looked to another and I saw his lips move. I watched more closely and was able to make out the words, "Head shot." My ability to read lips came in handy more often than not.

Fortunately, I had found a suitable hiding spot not far from the tree line. I was still in the shadows and thought I could chance a slow crawl for the short distance. When I reached the cover of the forest, I pressed the button on my company issued watch to let them know it was time for retrieval, then hiked my way out of there as fast as I could. The retrieval area was different than that of the drop off and I had several miles to cover before I made it out.

I trampled through the wilderness for hours, trying to cover my tracks, before I reached my destination. The chopper was hovering above the clearing with Black scanning the trees for my appearance. I stepped into the clearing and broke into a run toward the chopper. Black threw down a rope and harness then helped hoist me in. Brown had the chopper in motion before I was even inside.

My adrenaline rush didn't start to dissipate until we'd been in the air for thirty minutes. Between the three of us, nothing had been said so I decided to break the silence.

"So, what now?"

"We'll get back to the office and you'll be debriefed," Black answered.

The flight back wasn't nearly as long as the flight out. Having been alone for almost seven full days had taken its toll and I was so happy to be back, I almost gave this no thought. I checked my watch to be sure and was greeted with confirmation. I'd been patting myself on the back during the return flight and was pretty proud of myself. Now, with this discrepancy, I was reminded of the strangeness of the whole thing.

It didn't seem right that the company would send me on a sniping mission alone despite my intense training. I had never done anything like this before and I wasn't terribly confident and it showed. White and Associates didn't make mistakes and this could have easily been one. As I have said before, I wasn't thrilled with killing and I didn't make it a secret. However, I will admit, killing from a distance was much easier than face to face. Still, it seemed wrong to me that they would send me out on a mission of this type without some kind of backup, especially my first time out.

The man dropping to the ground before he should have kept replaying in my mind over and over as we entered the elevator to go to the 7th floor office. By the time we reached the office doors, I had convinced myself that something was definitely not right but I wasn't sure what exactly was going on.

Brown and Black escorted me to the office, one on either side of me. With the thoughts of something not being right and them standing so closely and quietly I was feeling especially tense. However, I didn't let it show on the outside. I had myself steeled for anything but I casually strolled into the office and saw White at his desk. Red was in a chair to White's left and Blue was also present, lounging on the comfortable couch.

Brown and Black left me in Whites office and shut the door behind them. Red gestured to one of the comfortable chairs and said, "Sit down, Ms. Grey. You have completed the mission?"

"Yes."

"We need the details."

I started with the hike to the compound and finished with the extraction and didn't leave out a single detail that had anything to do with the mission. I even admitted to not taking a shot the first time I saw the guy because the only identity confirmation I had was the mark on his hand. I was a bit afraid they might look down on me for that one, but this was a debriefing after all and they should know that I might not be cut out for this kind of work.

"Please excuse us for a moment," White dismissed me. "We won't be long so you can wait in the front office."

Gabriella was absent again today so I was alone. I wandered around nervously for about a minute before I forced myself to sit down and take some deep breaths. I wondered why I was so nervous about all of this. It must be because I always wanted to impress these men. There was something about them that made me want to fit into their group. However, something wasn't right about this mission. I started checking things off in my head. First I shouldn't have been sent on a job of this type without backup. Secondly, the briefing of the job was short and sweet and I didn't get anything from my partners about who this man was or why he needed to be taken out. Third, the timing, after I fired my weapon, just didn't seem right. I was thinking of the fourth reason, the shorter flight home, when the door opened and Blue asked me to step back into the office.

I reclaimed my seat from just a few moments ago and waited for whatever was coming next.

White rose from his seat and said, "This was a test, Alex."

I was surprised he called me by first name because he'd started the mission by using my company name. After my initial shock my first instinct was to stand and yell at them. If they are testing me they should tell me! Why would they not tell me? I resisted the urge to freak out and didn't let my anger show on my face.

"We wanted to see if you could do this type of job and we've come to the conclusion that you will do just fine if something comes up. Blue will walk you through the high points and low points of the mission."

I turned to face Blue who had resumed sitting on the couch. I was having a bit of trouble hiding my feelings but I managed to suppress the scowl when he started speaking.

"You did great. I'm thoroughly impressed. 'One shot, one kill' is exactly what you did." He paused. "First of all, let me explain a few things to you. The new laser sight I installed for you was actually how we knew where your bullet should have hit and of course, the bullets were blanks. You had mentioned seeing sensors on the targets face and that's exactly what they were. They were placed all over his body to capture your laser when you fired your gun."

"That explains why he fell before the bullet should have reached him," I interrupted, momentarily forgetting my anger.

"They were rigged with an alarm and he was to drop as soon as he heard it go off. We'll have to work on that for future testing."

Red cut in, "Not only that, the fact that you doubted the identity was a good thing. We will have to add that to the testing, too. A sniper should be, without a doubt, sure of who his target is."

"One thing I don't understand," White waited until we all turned to him. "I don't understand why you didn't ask more questions during the briefing. Why didn't you ask who the guy was and why didn't you ask why you were going to kill him? This is a man's life after all."

White and I had become very close over the past few months. I'd had only one friend my entire life, Colin DeLange. I never imagined I'd be as close to anyone like I was with Colin. Yet, somehow, White and I had forged a strong friendship and were rarely apart. If we weren't training or on a mission you could always find one by finding the other. But, with his last utterance, I hated him. I had been thinking the same thing since I first stepped onto the chopper to leave for this mission. He was right, I should have asked questions, but I trusted him. My poker face slipped and my feelings showed through. I let him have it. I've always had trouble hiding what I'm really thinking around White. If he just hadn't said anything, we probably would have all been happier people.

"I suppose I trusted you. Which is something I'll have to reconsider. I don't appreciate being tricked. I knew there was something wrong with this whole picture and it really makes me angry that you would take advantage of me in this way." I ranted for a little while longer before Red cut me off.

"Ms. Grey!" The shock of him yelling stopped me in mid sentence and he continued in a quieter voice. "This was not intended to trick you... well, not in the manner you interpret it. It was meant to test you and there is no better way to test you than if you think you are trying to complete a real mission." His voice was somewhat apologetic, but I couldn't tell you what his face looked like because I was staring at White. The corners of his mouth were turned up just enough for me to realize he was enjoying this, which made me even angrier.

My nostrils flared as I turned to look at Red. He didn't have the smirk White did, but he didn't show any regret in his face. I looked at Blue and he had the same expression. No remorse for what they had done to me. At some point in my rant, I had stood and that's what I was doing now. Standing there, with my fists clenched, fighting the urge to physically lash out at these men. I either had to try to kick their asses or relax and discuss this with them. They obviously thought they had done no wrong and maybe they hadn't. It was me who hadn't asked the questions. That wasn't like me. I always had questions to ask. Granted I didn't always ask the questions that were looming in my mind but when it came to something like this, I *should* have.

I gave each of them a glare and sat back down. I took a deep breath and waited for someone else to speak.

"Alex," White broke the uncomfortable silence, "this is how we do most of our training with our men. In fact, there were only a select few at the compound that knew you were out there. Not only were we testing you, we were testing some of our men. There is a valid reason behind this type of testing. We want our guys to do their best at all times. If they don't know it's not real, they will always try their best. We don't want anyone to get complacent. Do you understand that?"

"Yes, sir." My chin jutted out in defiance as I reverted to my Chief Slade training.

Red broke in, obviously trying to alleviate some of the tension. "Well, all in all, you did an excellent job. You completed the mission, you were not apprehended and they should still be searching for you if you covered your tracks the way you should have. But for now, this concludes the briefing. White has some info that the two of you should go through." He and Blue were obviously relieved as they left me alone with White.

Red had done some to pacify my ill temper, so after they left the room I was more open to hear what White wanted to say. In the short time since my outburst I'd thought of why they left me in the dark and realized my aggravation stemmed mainly from what I had failed to ask.

As White got up and went to the file cabinet in the corner of the office I told myself I wasn't really mad at him, I was mad at myself. The venom in my veins had subsided and then I became aware that White and I were alone. I'd become much more comfortable with White in the past months but my temperature always rose a few degrees when we were alone. Today was no different. I took a couple of deep breaths to calm myself even more. This helped and I was back to my normal outward self by the time he came back to his desk.

"So, how do you feel about the company, Ms. Grey?"

"Fine." White using my company name while we were alone was not lost on me. It was unexpected and had me a little worried. That aside, my reply was an understatement. I'd given some thought to going back to my former job but only because I missed the comforts of home, not because I wanted out. I loved the company. I am a restless person and the company scratched all of my itches. I was able to do things I would never have had the chance to do anywhere else.

"Good. It's time you learned more about us." He slid a large manila folder, overflowing with paper, across his desk.

"There's more to learn?" I picked it up and started flipping through it.

"Much more. You can look through it now or take it back to your apartment. It's up to you. I'll understand if you need more time to calm down."

I had entirely gotten over my anger until he said this and I looked up from the folder and saw that same smirk on his face. "I was calm, but you know just what buttons to push, don't you?" He laughed at me, which just fueled the flames. "Why do you enjoy making me mad?" I asked him in an even tone.

"I don't," his tone was one of total innocence, but he quickly changed back to his serious work attitude. "You will probably have some questions this time around. I can answer any of them, but you might find C.I.C. to be useful also." Then as an after thought he added, "I'm more than willing to go through all of this with you right now."

"If you don't mind, I'd like to go over it by myself first."

"Sure." I was already turned away from him but could still hear the smile in his voice.

# Chapter Two

I sat on the couch in my apartment reading and rereading the huge file. It was amazing what I didn't know about this company. I found myself flabbergasted more than once while combing through the material. Some of it seemed so obvious, yet I had let it slide right past me.

At one point a picture of Mr. Green, AKA Seth Caldwell, caught my attention. It was his dossier. It gave a brief background such as his date of birth, place of birth and parents' names. This information wasn't anything new. Then it became more detailed with his service record. It told me the date he had enlisted, his prior rank and job in the navy and a long list of commendations. It explained, in detail, his time with the Navy Seals. I flipped through all his information and came to a sheet labeled TEAM GREEN. Under the heading it read *Currently at 110* and this was followed by a long list of names. I started counting the names and decided the 110 meant people. I finished glancing at the names and moved onto the next file. Each partner was profiled and each partner had a team named for their color. I tallied up the numbers under the team headings and came up with over 1,000 people. Was this the size of the company?

White and Associates was a huge endeavor. It wasn't a company; it was an army. I had thought the company consisted of just the partners and some guys on the side who did the little jobs for us when we were busy or the jobs not important enough for us to get involved. Flipping through this material showed me how wrong I was.

I came to my dossier and there wasn't much on it. It simply stated my date of birth, place of birth, parents' names and "Trained under Master Chief Slade." I was a little ashamed to not have as good a resume as the others but at least I did also have a sheet titled TEAM GREY. Of course, there were no names on it.

I specifically looked up TEAM WHITE and was greeted with nothing but the partner's names. I decided it made sense so I continued to read the information in front of me. I noticed everyone's military rank as I read about him. I've never been good with military ranking but I did notice the chain of command. White had been the highest rank, then Black. Red and Blue were the same rank under Black, then Brown and then Green and finally me, with no rank at all.

I was fascinated by the material in front of me. I resisted the urge to call White because my previous outburst now had me feeling a little foolish. Instead, I got myself some paper and a pen knowing I wouldn't be able to remember all of my questions. I spent some time writing but eventually decided to give in and just call White.

He was available and at my apartment within minutes.

"So, got you interested, didn't I?" He uttered as I opened the door, a big grin on his face.

"Yeah," I grinned back at him.

The two of us sat on the couch and went through some of my questions. Before long, White suggested we make our way down to the War Room. That is what they affectionately called C.I.C., which stands for Central Intelligence Center and it was located in White's apartment. It housed several computers all linked to the national government and many other fun gadgets.

"Why do we have to go there?" I hadn't been in my apartment much for the past few months and was reluctant to leave it.

"We can call up satellite pictures and I can show you real time views of our compounds." He had talked me into it and we left my apartment and went to his.

White and Associates had several compounds in addition to the cabin and the building that housed our main office and our apartments. They all varied in size and location. I had White print out a picture of each compound so I could study them further.

After looking at the various compounds and having their purposes explained to me, I asked about the assorted teams I'd found in each partner's file. White went on to explain everyone had their specialty and each was assigned teams with the same strengths. For example, Blue was the company doctor so all the rest of the company doctors fell under him. Then White said that was a bad example because the doctors weren't always available to the company. They all had other practices and took jobs only as they were offered. A better example would be TEAM BROWN. Brown was an expert mechanic and pilot. Also, something that was news to me, Brown was an expert at demolition work. Therefore he had teams of mechanics, pilots and demolition experts at his disposal.

"But Blue is a sniper, too. Does he have sniper teams?" I had an interest in this due to my recent sniper training. I have to admit my mother's background played a part in my curiosity. I'd given the sniping test some thought and if killing was my only choice, I'd rather do it from a distance.

White's grin suggested he knew I'd ask about snipers. "Yes, he has twenty sniper teams consisting of two men, a sniper and a spotter." White described each partner's teams after that in full detail and then went on to tell me why I didn't have a team yet.

"We haven't decided your specialty. You show exceptional talent in many areas and it's hard to class you. However, with or without a specialty, you will be assigned a team."

"When?"

"Immediately."

"But if you haven't decided my specialty how can we assemble a team?"

"All the partners have teams with nothing but their specialty. We assemble squads as needed, for particular jobs. However, we should make these squads more permanent. The men will work better together if they've worked together in the past. I've decided to set up teams under you that encompass all the specialties," he paused. "You're teams will be," again he paused searching for the right words. "I suppose you could say they will be our elite."

White went on to explain my responsibilities to my teams. I was to make sure they worked well together and kept up on their training so they'd be prepared to take on jobs. Also, I'd be the one the rest of the partners would come to when they needed a team recommendation.

We spent the remainder of the night in C.I.C. going over my questions and wouldn't have known it was time for breakfast had Black not shown up at White's apartment. The room was windowless and time seemed to stand still inside.

"I've been trying to call you." He directed this at me as he walked into C.I.C. "Did you want to go to the gym today?"

"What time is it?" I began to notice my fatigue.

"A little after seven. I'm getting a slow start today."

"Can it wait a few hours? I haven't gotten much sleep these past few days." I yawned.

"We've been up all night going over the company business." White told him.

"How about tomorrow morning?"

"Sounds good. I think I'm going to go home and get some sleep."

When I reached my apartment I looked longingly at the shower but decided I was too tired and went straight to bed. I didn't wake until close to two in the afternoon. I immediately went in to shower, remembering how many days it had been.

As I showered I thought about the company and how differently I saw it now. I should have known there was more involved than I had been shown. My father was, after all, the reason the company was created. I should have known it wasn't a small operation.

Admiral Robert S. Stanton was not a man of small things. If he were involved, it had to be big. I began to kick myself once again for not realizing what I had been dealing with. I knew my father and these men well enough to know that this wasn't just a hobby. I had been given all the evidence and I didn't put it all together. "I should have known," I told myself over and over.

I thought back to the first time I saw Malone. I was twelve years old and my father had invited him and my best friend, Colin, and their fathers over to talk about possible military careers. My father has a high rank in the Navy and was friends with Colin's and Malone's fathers who were also military men. I've since learned that the talk that ensued that day was not only about getting Malone and Colin into the Navy, it was also about laying the ground work for White and Associates. That alone suggested something larger than my limited view of the company.

I'd thought of that day many times before, but in a different respect. That day, in my parents' back yard, I watched Malone and had my first epiphany. He had to be the man I would marry. I didn't see him again until that fateful day I walked into White and Associates to apply for a job. I hadn't forgotten the young man in my parents' back yard but didn't recognize White for who he really was until shortly after I started working with him. That was the direction my thoughts took every time I thought about that day. I made a conscious effort to connect the dots and knew I would think of that day very differently from now on.

When I applied for the job at White and Associates I didn't know what I was signing up for. I even thought the ad in the paper might have been for a cruise line. After I got the job, I learned that White and Associates is a PMC, or Private Military Corporation. Becoming a partner has been life changing, but I'm happy I've done it. It keeps me busy and interested, which can be a challenge. I am easily bored and that could be because I've been pampered all of my life.

Well, pampered might not be the right word, and I'm usually so good with words. All right, I'll call it like it is, even if I don't want to use the appropriate word. Spoiled would be more accurate. My parents have money and always have let me do what I want. For example, I'm an accomplished chef as well as proficient in many forms of fighting, thanks to Master Chief Slade. Mom and Dad's money paid for any training I was interested in and the training they thought I needed.

I went to college for computer science and walked away with a degree and the ability to do almost anything with a computer. I like to think that helped with me getting a job with White and Associates.

I've always worried that my father, being a founder of the company, is why I'm now a partner, but that's not entirely true. Mr. White is aware of my father's involvement in the company but is the only partner with such information. If any of the other partners had objected loudly enough, I wouldn't be a partner. I might have a job, but I wouldn't be a partner.

I am the only female partner and that also played a role in my quick elevation. The men needed a woman and I happened to be one. Again, my last name helped with their acceptance of me, but brought special emphasis to my skills. With the fact that my father's a high-ranking Naval Officer and very well known among the military community brings with it an expectation. He is now considered a civilian, but only for those who don't know what he really does.

He really works for the National Security Agency or NSA. That little realization didn't come to me until I took the job with White and Associates. But my father's job didn't come as much of a shock as my mother's true job. I always thought she was just my mom and my father's wife, but I was so very wrong about her.

She proved to be the notorious assasin, Penumbra. My father, White and I are the only people with the information of her true identity, as far as I know. I'm finding things are never what they seem. It's disheartening to discover you know much less about the world and people around you than you did when you woke up that morning. That, however, was the direction my life had been flowing for some time.

I first discovered my mother's secret identity more than six months ago, yet it still bothered me. The only thing I can think of is, I have a propensity for thinking I am uncommonly smart and when I am proven wrong, it stings a tiny bit.

I still believe my brain functions appropriately and I may have a little extra up there than some, but I am terribly naïve. I blame my parents for that. They kept me sheltered for most of my life. I was home schooled and didn't have much contact with the outside world until I went to college. Now, I'm in the real world and discovering how it all truly works.

As I got dressed I promised myself I'd be more diligent and observant of things around me. I didn't like being caught off guard and it had been happening at every turn lately. I planned to take more care with everything around me from now on; give things my full attention and take nothing for granted.

To start off right, I wanted to study the paperwork White had given me but remembered I'd left it in C.I.C. I immediately got on the phone and asked White if I could use C.I.C. again. He said he'd meet me at his apartment to let me in but he wouldn't be able to work with me right now.

I reached White's apartment before him and waited impatiently at his door. Eventually he made his appearance and let me into his apartment with instructions to lock up if I left before he returned.

I started researching and had several individuals in mind for teams but didn't know how to go about connecting them to a team until I knew more about them personally.

I typed up a list of people and their strengths and didn't take any breaks until it was time for dinner. After looking at the time, I decided to call it a night. I called Black and asked him if he'd like to join me at my apartment for dinner. He accepted the invitation and we spent the remainder of the evening eating and talking about my teams. He gave me some tips and pointed out things I had not even considered. I thought he would have helped me feel better about all of this, but I ended up going to bed that night worrying about my new assignment.

# Chapter Three

Black had given me instructions to call him as soon as I got up the next morning, but I allowed myself a shower and a cup of coffee first. When I finally called him, he immediately asked if I had coffee brewed and said he'd be right up.

After our quiet cup of morning coffee, the two of us made our way to Black's SUV in the parking garage. I hadn't been to a gym for several months and was hoping I wasn't too far out of shape. The last time Black took me to the gym he left to get us lunch and I had a line of sparring partners. I think everyone there wanted to try his or her luck against me. I chalked it up to my being new and smaller than most of them. I left that day with people still in line for their chance to take me down. I hoped today wouldn't be one of those days.

Black and I were greeted by Helix before the door shut behind us. I had forgotten about him. Helix is a big black man, with that deep voice that fits his size. He's the owner of the gym and apparently a good friend of Blacks.

The two men shook hands in the manner befitting of giants and then Helix turned his attention toward me.

"Still as fine as you was before, girl. You dump your man yet?"

"Thank you, no," I wasn't entirely comfortable with his attention and it must have shown.

"She's not your type, Helix," Black defended me.

"You sure it's not *him*?" He indicated Black as my boyfriend.

I just smiled and let it be. I didn't care who he thought I was dating and the bigger the better. I know Black would have him down in a matter of milliseconds and Helix knew that too. I think Helix could hold his own in the general world, but Black was trained better.

"Can we get a mat?" Black changed the subject.

"Of course. Follow me, my man."

Black and I squared off with each other and Black said, "He's harmless, I hope you know that." Then he lunged at me. I sidestepped and got in a good blow to his kidneys.

"I suppose. I'm just not all that comfortable with his demeanor." From then on we sparred without talking. After a two-hour workout, Black called an end to it.

"I can't get a hold of you and that's good, but it's frustrating."

We left the gym and sat in comfortable silence all the way back to the apartments.

I went straight to my shower then I called the office to check in. Gabriella answered and said I had a message from Colin. He had never left me a message at the office before. I was afraid it might be an emergency so I immediately called him back.

Colin was my first and best friend. He was the only person close to my age I knew when I was growing up. We spent most of our time together at our parents' houses. With what I have learned of my parents' backgrounds I understand why I was so sheltered, but I think Colin and I would still be best friends.

"Yo, Grey." Colin had taken to using my company name. I wasn't exactly sure how I felt about that, but I let it go.

"What's up?" I didn't hide the worry in my voice.

"I've got some news and wanted to know if you'd meet me for lunch," he said in an off hand manner but he couldn't completely hide his excitement.

"Sounds good. What's going on?"

"I'll tell you at lunch."

We made our plans and I hung up wondering what in the world could get him so excited that he would check the office for me. In a flash, a horrible thought entered my mind. Maybe he was getting married. I knew this day would come but I wasn't prepared for it yet. I still hadn't let go of my silly notion that I would marry Colin someday. I caught myself pacing around the room and forced myself to calm down. Sitting on my couch, I looked inward.

I remembered things we had done together, like trick or treating on Halloween or our training with Chief Slade and the long hours we spent together while Colin taught me sign language.

For most of my younger life I'd assumed I'd marry Colin. A girl's mind works a little differently than a boy's, I'm afraid. The first thoughts of boys usually include a castle, a prince, a kiss and finally, marriage. And Colin had always been my best and only prospect. He probably still is my best prospect, but no longer the only one.

He's got a good career in the Navy and would be my safest choice, but there was one other man in the running. Deep down I knew who was the "one" but the complications were immense. He was my boss, Mr. White, A.K.A. Rick Malone.

Thoughts of White soon overtook the thoughts of Colin being married and I knew my answer. I didn't want to let go of Colin, but I knew he wasn't the one. I wasn't entirely convinced White was the one either, but if he could replace Colin that easily, then Colin wasn't my soul mate. I felt better about letting Colin get married to some other woman, but now I worried that I wouldn't like her. Finally I told myself to shut up, I didn't even know if that's what he wanted to talk about. To get my mind on other things, I called White to find out when and how we'd make these teams a reality.

Gabriella told me he was in the middle of a call but I could come down and wait for him. She warned me that it could be a while because he had already been on the phone all morning. I didn't have anything else to do, so I thought I'd take her up on the offer.

I stepped into the office to hear Gabriella's upbeat voice say, "Hey hon!"

I greeted her and sat across from her at her desk. "Is White still on the phone?"

"Yeah, but that gives us a chance to talk. So, what do they have you doing now?"

"Nothing right now."

"Well, it's inspection time. I hate inspections. Everyone gets all serious." She stuck her tongue out. "That's why White's been on the phone. It also explains his attitude. He has barely said hello and certainly didn't ask me how my weekend went."

I caught the hint. "So, how did *your* weekend go?"

"I had a date." Immediately Mr. Black came to mind because she'd been drooling over him since before I joined the company. I just didn't figure Gabriella for his type of woman. She was a good ten years older than him and no matter how I tried, I couldn't see them as a couple. I had been gone much too long.

"With Black?" I tried to sound excited for her and not give away any shock.

"Nah, I gave up on him. He's too young for me anyway. This guy is something else though." She went on to tell me all about her weekend. Apparently the man was loaded or took out a small loan for their first date. Gabriella was thoroughly impressed with him. I sat there, glued to every description and found myself wishing I could find such a man. Maybe I should get out and date once in a while, I thought to myself. There was no point in waiting for White, even though it was entirely my fault he and I hadn't gotten together yet. I just wasn't ready for him but if I dated a couple of guys I'd be more prepared for White.

Eventually I glanced at my standard issue watch from White and Associates. It was one of those neat gadgets we got to play with once in a while. It came equipped with a GPS system and a homing beacon. I apologized for leaving in such a rush, but if I didn't hurry, I'd be late for my lunch date with Colin.

I practically ran to my car in the garage and sped out of there as fast as I could. I hadn't talked to Colin for a long time and I was looking forward to this but mainly, I was excited to hear his "news." I knew it had to be a big deal or he would have just told me over the phone. In my rush to get to the restaurant I missed the turn. I got turned around and as soon as I entered the parking lot I found a spot.

I hurried myself inside only to find that Colin hadn't arrived yet but had made a reservation. The girl led me to our table and left me there with a menu, a glass of water and my thoughts.

I sat alone wondering, again, what could be so important to Colin. Soon my mind wandered off course and started following its normal path of thinking. My fantasy life began at age twelve after seeing White. Since then, he'd been my main fantasy, but now I had a name and an attitude to put into the daydreams. However, the attitude didn't always play too well with what I had in my mind. Before long I was angry with White and wondering where in the world Colin was. I checked my watch.

The third time I looked up from checking my watch I saw Colin being led to our table by the same girl who had deposited me there more than four minutes earlier. I never said patience was an asset of mine. It was a wonder I didn't go crazy during the sniper training.

He was grinning from ear to ear and I stood up to greet him with a hug. "I've missed you," he said as he squeezed me tighter than normal.

"What's going on?" My interest was piqued and it came through in my voice. Colin was always glad to see me but his enthusiasm was bubbling over.

"I haven't seen you for such a long time. I do have news, but can't your best friend be happy to see you without something being 'up'?"

"Not this happy."

"Fine. You know me too well. Let's sit down and it'll be explained soon. We can catch up before everyone else shows up."

"Everyone else?" I questioned as we took our seats.

"Yes, two other people are going to join us. We could have done this without you, but we thought it best if you were here when it happened than if we were there when *you* found out about it later." His grin got even bigger, if that was possible. He was starting to remind me of Mr. Brown, who always had a smile on his face.

"Tell me. What's going on and who else is coming?"

"So, what have you been doing?" He ignored my questions.

We spent the next fifteen minutes talking about what I'd been doing for the past three months. Colin and I hadn't had contact for several months but we always fell right back into the swing of things. I gave him the brief version of my sniper training and the other minor jobs I'd been involved in. I used to wonder when my training would end but now I knew it was an ongoing thing that never ended for any of the partners or employees of White and Associates.

He then told me he'd been promoted to the rank of Lieutenant Commander. This came as a shock. I got easily confused when it came to the military ranking system, but I knew this was five or six pay grades above Colin's last rank.

"How did you manage that?"

"Hard work, and knowing your father is always an asset," he shrugged his shoulders.

"So, you didn't entirely deserve this? Is that what you're telling me?"

"No, I deserve it. Knowing your father can also be a detriment," to this he smiled. "He had put in a word to hold back my advancement. I don't know why yet, but I imagine we will find out today."

"Oh, so it's my father who's going to be joining us? Who is the second person?"

"White."

"White? Why?" My mind was working over time trying to see the connection and then it hit me. White had explained my father's master plan for White and Associates months ago. White was to head up the PMC end and Colin was to head up the government connection of the equation when my father felt Colin was ready for it. "Oh," I let my voice trail off.

"Yep, I am now a part of your life again." I could tell Colin was working hard to restrain himself. I'm sure he wanted to jump up and down with glee and probably had already, in private. This was what he had gone into the military for, to help my father with an outside agency that could get things done that the government didn't dare touch.

"So, this means you are a higher rank than Master Chief Slade." I was still adjusting to the thought.

"I never thought of that, but yeah, I am." I could literally see his ego swelling.

"You better be careful. I've found that things like this rarely come without a high price, especially when White and my dad are involved."

"Let me enjoy this while I can. I know I'm going to have to work even harder now, but I have to get the bragging out of my system before Admiral Stanton and White show up."

"Probably a good idea."

Colin said this a few seconds before White was led to our table.

"The Admiral isn't here yet?" White said by way of greeting.

"Not yet," I replied.

Colin's demeanor changed in the few seconds it took for White's voice to reach his ears. He became more serious and the smile on his face lessened. There had always been friction between the two of them. I didn't know the history, but I assumed it had to do with Colin taking my fathers place in the company and White being promoted before Colin and seemingly being more "in charge."

Now things were about to change and I didn't know how I felt about it all. The other partners did not know about my father, Admiral Stanton, and his role in the company, but was that going to remain the same with Colin? I had noticed that the men didn't have much respect for Colin and I think the only reason for that was because he was younger than all of them.

White took a seat next to mine and across the table from Colin.

"White," Colin nodded his hello. I'd never heard him call White anything other than Malone. This was a new show of respect from Colin.

"Commander," White replied respectfully, then smiled a greeting to me. The three of us sat quietly, waiting for the Admiral.

My father's arrival came within a few minutes of White's, which was a relief. I didn't know how much longer I could sit in silence with all this new information rattling around in my brain.

"I'm assuming we are all aware of what is going on except for maybe Ms. Grey," was my father's greeting to us all as he sat. His attitude was somewhat detached and businesslike.

"I'm sure she knows, Admiral," White informed him.

I nodded my confirmation so the meeting could move on.

"First, Ms. Grey, you must know the reason you were invited to be a party to this meeting. DeLange and White would not have allowed this meeting to be held without your attendance. I, personally, think it's disgraceful to be afraid of a woman, but then again, I am reminded of who your mother is," he succeeded in lightening the mood that had pervaded since White had joined our little party. I didn't know if Colin knew the true significance of that statement but it didn't really matter anyway.

He then began the meeting by telling us that Colin was still working his way up the ladder and him taking his place in the company depended upon his acceptance into the Naval Intelligence Service or NIS. He explained to us all that he had made sure Colin's rank was withheld because he wanted to see if Colin would continue to work toward the goal of taking his place, even if it didn't seem like it would be coming any time soon. He talked more of Colin's role as well as what would be expected of the rest of the partners. He questioned White about the rest of the company and their possible rejection of Colin but White assured him everything would be fine and added, as long as the arrangement remained the same as in the past.

"Of course Colin's involvement in the company will be known to only us, except in the event of a job offering. However, White, I do hope you realize *everything* will remain the same, except for the person you will be dealing with." The conversation turned toward the monetary aspect of the company.

I learned a few things, such as my father received a percentage of every transaction that White and Associates completed. I assumed this already but Colin was now in a position to be receiving half of this commission.

"Of course, Admiral. He will receive his cut. He's one of us now." Surprisingly, White didn't seem all that concerned.

Then my father asked White if there would be any problems taking jobs from Colin.

"No, Admiral. I am actually looking forward to working with DeLange as well as I'm sure Ms. Grey is." I had to fight against a compelling urge to roll my eyes, but I succeeded. Maybe they'd already gotten past whatever had caused the past friction.

The Admiral gave me a strange look but continued, "Good because he has a job proposal for you."

Colin took over the meeting and explained the job he wanted White and Associates to accept. "The job is for information. There will be no contact with the targets. As you know, five years ago Dimitri Glaskov passed away." White nodded his head and so did I. Dimitri was the head of one branch of the Russian mafia. His death was in all the newspapers because it was especially gruesome. A wood chipper was found dismantled and scattered along the highway. Inside they found a couple of human teeth that turned out to belong to the notorious mafia boss.

"Dimitri's son, Grigori, is now believed to have taken Dimitri's place at the head of this branch," he paused briefly.

"Grigori has a reputation for extravagance but toned down his act shortly after the news of his father's death. According to some of our sources, Grigori has engaged in several meetings with an older man these past months. These meetings have all been very private until recently. They have taken to meeting at a local club that Grigori owns called The Rave. We've been unable to find out anything substantial because the club is so loud. I thought Grey's ability to read lips could come in handy here." Colin's mother was deaf so, in trade for special training from Master Chief Slade, he'd tutored me in sign language and lip reading for as long as I could remember. I'd gotten much better at lip reading over the past year because I knew it had other applications besides hearing about the neighborhood gossip.

"Sounds easy enough," White told Colin.  Of course it sounded easy enough, he wasn't the one going to be working the job. I knew I could do it though so I kept my mouth shut. White and Colin worked out all the details including White and Associates compensation for this particular job.

"Good enough," my father stood from the table, signaling the end of the meeting. After he shook hands with both men he scolded me for not coming home to keep Mom up to date. According to him, she was constantly speculating on what I was doing. I promised to give her a call as soon as I could and reached over to give him a kiss.

After the Admiral left us, White stood and stuck his hand out at Colin,

"I'm happy for you and look forward to our first job together. Be seeing you, Commander. As for you, Grey, I expect to see you in the office later today."

Colin stood and shook White's hand, said thank you and then told me he needed to get back as well. Within seconds I was left alone in the restaurant with no lunch, a glass of water, a menu and my thoughts.

I really didn't want to eat lunch alone, but I was hungry and was left with no other choice. When the waitress returned to take our orders she only received mine. I felt like everyone was watching me so I ate quickly and left.

I was back at the office in record time and found Gabriella at her desk.

"Is White in?"

"Yep, he said to let you in whenever you showed." She smiled.

"Thanks," I said as I opened White's office door.  He was sitting at his desk looking intently at some paperwork. I shut the door behind me and he looked up.

"Hi. I didn't expect you here so soon."

"I really don't have anything else to do." I sulked.

"Really? Well, I can fix that." He grinned at me. "First, what do you think of Colin 'taking over'?"  Just as quickly as the smile appeared it disappeared.

"See? I knew you'd have a problem with this."

"I don't have any problems with it... Okay, that's not true, I don't know exactly how to handle DeLange being my boss." He sighed.

"My father isn't really your boss so why would Colin be? Once, you told me when the Admiral brought you jobs you could refuse them."

"But, I also told you that I probably shouldn't refuse to take them."

"So, you think Colin will be able to tell you what to do? That's what bothers you?"

"Yes and no," he frowned. "I shouldn't be talking to you about this."

"Why not? Who else are you going to talk to about it? Do any of the guys know the deal you struck with my dad and Colin?"

"No, but *Colin* is your best friend."

"So, you think I'm going to run to him and tell him all about this conversation?"

"I don't know. Are you?" He questioned me.

"White, you're a jerk. You just don't get it yet, do you?" I was offended by his comment. Did he really think I would run to Colin with company business? I don't know if I would hide anything from Colin, if asked, but if it came from White, I probably would.

"Get what?"

"I am part of this company and I don't see that changing any time soon. When it comes to this kind of thing, my first obligation is to White and Associates." I put special emphasis on the White and he raised his eyebrows.

"I guess you're right. I can be a jerk. I'm sorry, I suppose it's because of the job I hold. It's hard to trust people."

"Do you trust Black?"

"With my life."

"Then why can't you trust me?"

"I do, but..."

"But what?" Now I was getting aggravated.

"Your father is pretty much my boss and your best friend is going to take his place. Actually, you probably have more pull in this company than I do."

"Now you're just feeling sorry for yourself. You know better than all that. My father has less faith in me than you do and Colin still sees me as his friend, who's a girl. Do you think part of your problem is he's going to outrank you in the military."

"That doesn't bother me. I'm not in the military anymore. I see your point about DeLange not really being my boss too. It's not always been this way.  We used to be pretty good friends but several years ago..." he let it hang there.

"What happened?" I asked after a long pause.

"We've talked about this before and I used to think it was because of my quick elevation.  But, I'm not really sure.  We'll see how things progress now that he's actually getting somewhere with his career." he shrugged it off.  "First things first.  We'll complete this job and see how it goes," then he changed the subject.  "Have you decided on any teams?"

"Actually, I have.  I just don't know if they'll work well together until I talk to them, or see them in action."

"I figured we'd have to do interviews anyway.  Inspections are going on right now and I planned on sending you to visit the compounds.  It'll be good for the men to see you and for you to familiarize yourself with the company.  Go over your list and let me know which compound you want to visit first."  He concluded our meeting by telling me to go get ready for Colin's job and stressed that he wanted me to decide on a compound as quickly as possible so he could make arrangements.

# Chapter Four

Later that afternoon, Black showed up for coffee. I told him I was going to be leaving soon to start interviews and I needed to tell White which compound I wanted to go to.

"And?" he asked.

"There aren't too many candidates at the Alaskan compound but I've always wanted to see Alaska." I shrugged.

"I have to tell you, the average temperature for this time of year is only 40 degrees at our Alaskan compound. But it beats the rest of the year," he took a sip of his coffee.

I really wanted to see Alaska so I made my decision final by calling White at the office.

"Damn it! I didn't want to go there," he complained.

"I have a couple of picks at that compound I'd like to interview."

"Well, if you make any team picks I'll want to review them. Besides, I won't send you off to the compounds alone until the men know you. I think you should have a senior partner with you at each compound you visit. It could be a disaster to drop you off at a compound without one of us to back you up."

"What do you mean, back me up? Don't you think I can take care of myself?" I resented his attitude.

"That's not it. It will just be easier for everyone involved if you have one of us with you on your first visit to each compound."

"All right. I can see your point," I conceded. "What time are we leaving to do the job for Colin?"

"In a few hours, so be ready." White hung up without a good-bye.

"So?" Black asked as I replaced the receiver.

When I told Black that White wasn't all that happy about having to go to Alaska, he grinned. Then I quickly outlined our previous conversation with the Admiral and Colin. I told him I was to meet White at the office in a few hours. He gave me a nod and said he'd see me at the office later.

The rest of my day was occupied with finding an appropriate clubbing outfit. I wanted to fit into the crowd but still be comfortable enough in my clothes that I could do anything... just in case.

Black collected me a few hours later and we made our way to the office.

"I'm glad you're both here." White waved us to our seats. "Let's begin the briefing."

White told us that we were going to a club called The Rave. Grigori was expected to have a meeting with the elusive man again. Of course, my job was to read their lips and White and Black would be there to make sure I stayed out of trouble.

We walked into the Rave and the music hit me like a wall. It made my body tremble and my heart flutter. It had a deepness that you could feel to your toes and all I wanted to do was dance. It was trancelike. The people closed in around us. I didn't know how we were supposed to spot our target in this mess of moving bodies and flashing lights. I fought the urge to let the music take me and started scanning the room, looking back to make sure White and Black were still right behind me. Both of them were exactly where they should be, if they were bodyguards, and I had a small opening around me because of it. I should go everywhere with these two, I thought.

"I could get into this," I yelled to White over the music. This was somewhat like a massive house party and much bigger than anything I had ever experienced.

He grabbed his ear with the earpiece in it and grimaced. "They can be fun." He yelled back at me after he regained his composure.

As I scanned the crowd I caught sight of a balcony. I pointed to it and Black took my arm and led the way. White took my other arm and trailed behind me. As we moved, the crowd squeezed in on us, threatening to break us apart. We reached the top and I watched as Black looked over the crowd on the balcony and White looked out over the sea of people below us. I did the same and found it hard to pick a face out of the crowd. Before long, Black nudged me and discretely pointed toward the back wall. Then he and White moved away from me to watch out over the crowd below.

I turned and noticed the back wall was lined with cubicles of different sizes and bathed in soft pink lights. To make the picture perfect, the rooms were curtained with sheer drapes. Near Grigori was a bottle of brandy, an ice bucket, and one glass. It must have been meant for a guest because he sipped a martini.

He held his drink in one hand and a large cigar in the other. There was a woman rubbing his shoulders and another was under his arm with the cigar. She was secretly trying to blow the smoke far away. I found it comical. One minute she was smiling and the next she was blowing air out the side of her face. Four other large men stood scattered about. Their eyes constantly roamed the room and the crowd outside.

Within minutes another man somewhere between forty something and sixty something appeared outside the room. He brought with him his own bodyguards. He waited impatiently as Grigori dismissed his girls. Soon both men were seated in heavily pillowed couches surrounding the small table. Grigori poured the man a glass of brandy.

Before we came inside, White had fitted me with a choker necklace that had a microphone and transmitter in it. He said it would work well because it was directly on my throat so my voice would come through better than the background music.

I started repeating everything I saw the men say and hoped it was getting through to Colin and Red outside in the van. It was a challenge to see their lips clearly through the drapes but I managed. Both White and Black were wearing earphones and Black gave me confirmation from across the room that it was getting through with a nod of his head.

"Grigori," the older gentleman said as they shook hands and accepted the glass offered him. It seemed oddly bold that he'd speak to the head of the Russian Mafia so informally. "You know I'm not happy meeting here. What is so important?"

"Yes, *ah chets*." I didn't know what Grigori had said and repeated what I thought I'd seen. As soon as I said it, I felt foolish. It didn't make any sense. My mind was taken off my mistake for a split second as I watched Grigori scoot deeper into the couch with a look of horror. The older gentleman's reflexes were spectacular. He reached over and slapped Grigori across the face hard enough to make his nose bleed. Grigori's men flinched at the contact and started making their way to the other man. Grigori waved them away and took a handkerchief out of his jacket pocket to wipe away the blood. I was kicking myself for not catching what was really said. This was important and I'd screwed it up.

"Never again, you careless..." the man stopped, his face red.

"Yes, Mr. Prutko. Please, forgive me." Grigori looked crushed but continued. "I was hoping to show you what you could expect in the near future. I have acquired Gigi's for you."

The men didn't speak again for several minutes and I was beginning to get restless.

I glanced at White. He mouthed, "Watch."

"If you are unable to control your tongue we will no longer be able to meet in public." Mr. Prutko spoke up, his composure completely restored.

"Of course," Grigori agreed. "I have all the paperwork for you to sign right here," one of the bodyguards handed him a folder. Mr. Prutko seemed unashamed of his lack of civility while he signed the paperwork.

White interrupted my view.

"I think we should reposition you for a little while."

"Why? What if I miss something?"

"We don't want you to be noticed any further," he indicated one of the bodyguards. "He's been watching you watch Grigori for a while now. We need to move along or risk a problem."

I shrugged my shoulders and followed him back down the stairs.

Since I couldn't do my job right now, I focused my attention on the crowd and the music. I was thoroughly enjoying myself when Black poked me in the side. It startled me because he had come up beside me when I wasn't looking.

"Quit singing. It's all I can hear." He hollered.

I was instantly embarrassed and shot White a guilty look and he was openly grinning. I hadn't given any thought to the choker and didn't realize Black and White would be hearing me too. That must be why White grabbed his ear earlier when I screamed at him that I liked this place. I didn't sing anymore, but I couldn't stop myself from moving, just the tiniest bit, to the entrancing music.

It wasn't too long before I got antsy and I asked quietly, "Can we go back?" The thought of the missed words was starting to weigh heavily on me and I wasn't enjoying the music as much as before.

White's lips moved, "No need, Prutko's on his way out."

He turned his head and I followed his gaze. Prutko walked importantly toward the exit.

After he exited the building White walked away only to come back five minutes later with a drink.

"What are you doing?" I was shocked he'd go get himself a drink while we were on a job.

"I was asked to retrieve this for Colin," he held up the glass and pointed at his earpiece. "Cost me three-hundred dollars," he said loudly into my necklace. The combination of his breath on my neck, his smell, and the music was enough to make my knees wobble. I pushed him away from me and gave him the best disapproving look I could manage in my state.

The three of us piled into the van and Red promptly had me backed into a corner asking me about the words I'd missed.

"Watch my lips. Could it have been Отец?" He said it slowly and it sounded like atyets.

"Say it faster. You're exaggerating your mouth, just say it like you normally would." I ordered and Red complied. "Yes. I think that's what it was. What does it mean?"

"It's Russian for 'father'," he glanced at Colin who was beaming at our discovery.

"Here," Colin handed a wad of cash over to White. "That's out of pocket expenses. You'll receive the rest of the payment in the usual manner. Now, give me that glass."

I'd seen pictures of Dimitri Glaskov and Mr. Prutko shared a small resemblance, but could it really be him.

"Does this mean that was really Dimitri in there?" I couldn't hold it in any longer.

"We won't be sure until we get this glass tested for DNA but I've suspected it for months now," Colin was still grinning happily.

The remainder of the drive back to the office was uneventful and I felt much better that I hadn't really screwed anything up.

I awoke early the next morning and Black was at my door before the coffee was done brewing. He immediately went to the coffee pot and started to pour himself a cup.

"You're spilling." I pointed to the puddle on the counter.

Black put the pot back into its place with a quick motion and grabbed a towel.

"Sorry."

"What are we going to do about Dimitri?" I asked, taking a seat next to him at my kitchen bar.

"Nothing."

"What? Why?"

"We haven't been hired to do anything about him."

"So, do you think we will be hired for anything?"

"Doubt it."

I didn't bring the subject up again until we were at the gym working up a sweat. Black cut me off, saying it wasn't our problem.

This wasn't good enough for me so when we got home I went directly to White's office.

Gabriella was in her seat so I spent a short amount of time visiting with her. She had fresh, long stemmed roses on her desk. Her new man was true to form. He'd spent a fortune on another date. I pictured myself on a date with White. He came to my door and escorted me to the car and held my chair at the restaurant. Everything a gentleman would do. Then I was abruptly pulled from my daydream by Gabriella's voice.

"What's wrong, hon?"

"Oh," I realized I'd been staring into White's office. "Nothing. I'd just love to go out on a date like that. Just once."

"You need to get out. Take some time off," her voice trailed off. "Would you be interested in a double date?" She asked suddenly with a twinkle in her eye.

"Uh," I fumbled. At least she hadn't noticed where I'd been staring. "I don't know."

"I'll get it set up. Don't make any plans for tonight." She beamed at me.

"Gabriella, I don't know. I don't know what White wants me to do," I tried to get out of it.

"I'll take care of everything. Now get in there and find out what *he's* got planned for you and tell him you're busy tonight."

I tried to object but she was very insistent as she shoved me toward White's office.

"I'm glad you stopped by," White greeted me as I stumbled in. "I want you to spend some time with Red before we leave for Alaska."

"Okay. Why?" I wasn't expecting this. I'd thought he might have a job for us concerning Dimitri.

"It won't hurt for you to get a little more formal training in leadership. Plus he'll help you go through the records to set up some teams."

"Fine, but what about Dimitri? Has my dad or Colin said anything to you about him?" The double date had left my mind.

"Nope and I doubt they will. Not yet anyway."

"They haven't even talked to you about anything?" I was bothered about being left in the dark over such a serious matter.

"No," his voice was slow and steady. "They won't either. That's none of our business unless they choose to hire us for something. We got more information than they expected though, so I'm sure they are happy with last night's job."

"Fine." I understood where he was coming from. My curiosity didn't fade but I decided to let it drop for now.

Gabriella stopped me on my way out, reminding me of the date she wanted to set up.

"I don't think I'll be able to do it," I started to say when she interrupted me.

"It's all set. You can come home with me after work and get ready at my house. It'll be so much fun," she gushed. "Us girls, going on a date. I can do your makeup..." she went on like this for several minutes before ushering me out the door to go find a suitable outfit.

She informed me she'd be up to check my choices after work so I better have some set out.

I'd never had a girl friend before and this was all so different. Colin had never wanted to do my makeup or nails. He had pointed out some guys to me, but only in fun. He'd never actually set me up with anyone. I didn't know how to react to all of this so when I got back to my apartment I gave him a call. I wanted to talk to him about Dimitri anyway.

I started the conversation with questions about Dimitri but he quickly put a stop to it. He said they hadn't even gotten the DNA tests back and even if they had he wasn't sure what they were going to do. I tried to argue with him but he wouldn't budge so I changed the subject.

"It'll be good for you," he said after I explained my plight. I thought he'd be on my side. "Anthony never treated you right and it'll be good for you to have a man treat you to dinner."

"I don't even know who these men are," I protested.

"I doubt Gabriella is dating a murderer with that kind of money." He laughed. "Here's what you do," he explained. "Hack into the system and look up the men Gabriella is taking you to meet. If you find them, maybe you should steer clear. If not, take your chances. If nothing else, you'll have a night out," he paused. "How long has it been?" I could hear the villainous grin through the phone.

"You're no help," was all I could manage.

I went to my closet and started rummaging. I didn't want to go slinky for a first date and I didn't want to go too conservative either. Three dresses lay on my bed before I became aware that I was enjoying myself and was actually looking forward to meeting someone new.

Pulling myself up short, I sat on my bed with my head in my hands. I knew I wanted to go on a date and be treated like a lady. Move back into the land of real people instead of the land of White and Associates. I really loved my job but I did need a break, some time for me to do something different. Going on a date was certainly different to me. Part of me wished it were with White but a wave of panic swept over me with that thought. This might be best, I told myself. White was the perfect man, as far as I was concerned, but I wasn't ready for the perfect man, yet.

I started trying on the different outfits and was scrutinizing myself in the mirror when a knock at my door startled me. A tiny squeak escaped as I gave a slight jump. I looked around guiltily and thought about changing back into my daily clothes but then my doorbell rang.

I opened the door to Red who was keenly taken aback by my appearance. I felt myself blush as he walked past me into my apartment.

"Uh, White asked me to get together with you." He was very uncomfortable.

"I'm sorry. I didn't know you were coming. Gabriella wants me to go on a double date with her tonight," I explained my dress.

"Oh." He'd been turned away from me but turned toward me obviously relieved with my statement. "You look very nice."

"Thank you. But I'm going to go change now." It hit me why he'd been so rattled. He thought I'd dressed up for him. As if.

I was redressed in my ordinary clothes in record time and found Red sitting at the bar in my kitchen.

"Better?" I asked, peeved that he was so put off that I might want to look nice once in a while.

"Less startling," he said. "You *do* make an impression in a dress. So, you have a date?" He saved himself.

"A blind date," I shrugged. "Gabriella kind of side-swiped me."

"She does have a way about her. Lets go through this, shall we?" He indicated the file folders he'd brought with him and had laid out neatly over my counter top. All talk of my date ended and we poured over employee records. He had a file for each specialty. We put together teams of the best we had with at least one of each skill.

"These men will be cross trained," Red explained as he started gathering his paperwork. "Most of them have had some type of cross training but we are going to go into more depth now that we have teams set up."

"How will we know if they work well together?"

"You'll do some interviewing but the only way to know is to put them on a job."

"Do we really want to take that chance? Shouldn't we test them first?"

"You're learning," Red smiled. "Yes. We will test them. White will set that up but in the meantime you will be going around to interview the men. We can force them into these teams but would rather give them the opportunity to join them willingly. It'll be your job to convince these men to be promoted. It *is* a promotion so it should be easy enough, however, some might need some convincing."

I nodded my understanding and stood from my chair to see Red out. He glanced toward my bedroom, seeing my dresses on the bed.

"May I?" He indicated my room.

"I guess."

"I don't want to be pushy, Alex. But, I know what goes on in this company and I know you've been with us for over a year now and have not had a single date. If you don't mind, I do have a little insight on a man's mind. Plus I do also know a little about human behavior."

"Okay," I was still reluctant as I followed him to my bedroom.

He gave the dresses on the bed a once over and asked where we were going.

"I don't know. I don't even know the name of Gabriella's boyfriend, let alone the name of my date."

"Call Gabriella and find out. You can't decide what to wear if you don't know what you'll be doing."

I did as I was told and came back to him with my information.

"Dinner at the Maddison Hotel. I guess Gabriella's date, Martin, owns the place. I'm going to be set up with his little brother, Leland. Then we are supposed to go dancing afterward." My stomach flipped as I relayed this to Red.

"Sounds like fun. Okay, you need something that invites a man's eyes but not his hands. Something upscale for the Maddison and something you can move in for dancing." He might know what he was talking about after all. This might not be so bad.

Red dismissed the dresses I'd already chosen and went straight for one of my favorites that I had never worn because I'd never been anywhere I felt it would be appropriate. It was a dark blue that made my skin look very pale.

"You don't think this color would make me look sickly?"

"Hmmm," he considered. "Try it on real quick." He left my room, shutting the door behind him.

Again, I did as I was told and glanced at myself in the mirror. I didn't look as bad as I'd remembered. I'd gotten some sun these past few months I guess. When I opened the door Red nodded his head in approval.

"This is nice," he reached for me and stopped his hands just before he made contact. "The neck is high but the shoulders are exposed. Having the neck covered is a good way to say that you are not accessible and mix that with exposed shoulders and it says 'Look but don't touch.' Am I getting your mood right?"

"Yes. I don't want some guy I don't know fondling me." I felt my cheeks color at my outburst. It had never been my intention to tell Red anything personal, ever. He and I had a rocky start and had never recovered. I wasn't sure I wanted to be having these conversations with Red. He was a psychiatrist after all and I didn't need him analyzing my sex life.

"Well, it's decided then. Get your bag and I'll walk you to the office. Gabriella is off in about five minutes."

"She was going to meet me here," I reminded him.

"Do you want her to make you change your clothes? Or spend an hour up here trying to pick out what you should wear after you've already done it?"

"I see your point. I'll meet you at the elevator." Red might not be as bad as I thought.

The elevator ride was slightly strained as we both stood stiffly in the car. My demeanor had softened a little toward Red but my nervousness for my date put us both on edge.

He held the doors while I exited and followed closely behind me as I sashayed into the office. It was unintentional but the dress required a certain walk.

Gabriella gave out a squeal and White looked up from his desk. I saw his jaw drop and felt the heat of his eyes on me as he slowly rose from his desk to come see what the fuss was about.

"You are beautiful!" Gabriella raved and pulled my attention from the slowly advancing White. "What am I supposed to wear now? I don't have time to go shopping." She was visibly torn between admiring me and cursing me for showing her up.

"Red helped me pick it out." He was still standing behind me so he didn't see my raised eyebrows.

"Red, you dog! Why do you want to do this to me?" Gabriella chided him.

"Alex deserves a night out." I had moved to see Red's face. His reply was clearly meant for White as well as Gabriella.

"Why so dressed up, Ms. Grey?" White interrupted.

I turned back to see him sizing me up from his doorway. My internal temperature skyrocketed but I was able to keep the flush from my skin.

"Gabriella talked me into a double date," I said a little sheepishly.

"She's been pining over my date descriptions so I thought I'd do her a favor and get her out there again," Gabriella hadn't felt the tension. "Dinner and dancing," she went on about how much fun we were going to have and I didn't hear most of it because of White's eyes. They were a mixture of amusement, bitterness, hunger and anger, if I was reading him right. I adverted my gaze and put all of my attention on Gabriella as she grabbed her things and led me out of the office, still jabbering about the impending date.

The two of us entered the elevator and her tone changed immediately.

"Did you see the look on White's face?" Her one-eighty surprised me.

"No?" I played dumb.

"Come on girl. You don't really think I'm that dense do you?" She leveled a serious look at me.

"No. I don't think you're dense," I was going to continue to play dumb.

"Then don't think I don't know what's going on between you and White." Thankfully the elevator doors opened and she led me to her car in the parking garage.

I was dreading the conversation after we got into the car and wasn't disappointed.

"This will be good for him too," she informed me. "I see the way the two of you look at each other and he needs to make a move. If he sees you moving on with your life it might just knock some sense into that boy!"

I was flabbergasted and sat in the passenger seat trying to keep my mouth in a closed position.

"You do need a night out anyway," she reached over and moved the hair out of my eyes, almost motherly. "Don't think about White tonight. Lets have fun!" She cranked up the radio and started singing loudly.

'Don't think about White tonight.' Who was she kidding? With the looks I received in the office and her cornering me on my feelings for him, how could I think of anything else? Was I really that obvious and if White was that obvious why didn't I see it? He'd told me before that he was interested but I just couldn't believe he was interested in more than just the physical. Gabriella had warned me away from him right away. Now she was making moves to make him jealous. I wondered what had changed.

I tried to bring the subject up while she was painting my nails an appropriate color for my dress and she waved it away. "I said not to think about White tonight. Tonight is for you." She started to brag up Martin and I got lost in her descriptions again and White eventually moved to the back of my mind.

"Are you nervous?" she asked as a limo pulled into her driveway.

"Yes," I admitted. "I've never been on a real date before and never a blind date."

"Well, I don't know Leland at all so you stay close to me and Martin. Unless you want to be alone with Leland," she wagged her eyebrows at me and I found myself grinning back at her.

"Shouldn't we go?" I asked as the limo came to a complete stop in front of her garage.

"Are you kidding? They need to come collect us. Besides, I want to meet Leland on my own turf before I let you go out on a date with him."

Shortly after her comment her doorbell rang. She instructed me to sit down and look bored while she went to the door.

Martin gave her a soft kiss and then introduced Leland to her. She allowed them inside so I assumed Leland was to her liking so far.

Martin stepped in first. He was semi paunchy and balding but he had an alluring twinkle to his eyes. Upon first glance I liked him. He stuttered a soft hello to me as Gabriella introduced us then introduced me to his younger brother Leland.

Leland was similar to his brother without the extra weight and slightly more hair. However, he lacked the friendly twinkle in his eyes. Instead he wore a shrewd look. Martin seemed taken with me but Leland was strangely aloof, as if I might not be good enough for him. I became even more worried about the rest of the evening.

The men escorted us to the limo and let us climb in first. Gabriella sat opposite me so she could be near Martin and I near Leland. She gave me a questioning look as we drove to the restaurant. She an Martin had been talking while Leland and I sat quietly on our side of the limo. Leland had been staring out the window at the passing scenery.

Thankfully the ride was short. Before long the four of us were being seated for our meal.

Things lightened up some as we ate and drank. Leland actually told a couple of stories and smiled three times. The food and wine was some of the best I'd ever had and I forgave Martin for ordering for the whole table.

Gabriella said she needed to powder her nose and gave me a look that said I needed to as well. The men rose from their seats as we did and remained standing until we rounded the corner for the restroom.

"So?" Gabriella pointed to a lattice wall. I looked through it and saw Martin and Leland at the table talking.

"It's going okay," I shrugged as I looked back at her.

"No, silly. What are they saying? I know you can read lips. Hurry up, don't miss anything." She physically turned me back around and practically pushed my face into the lattice.

"She's okay," I saw Leland say.

"What do you mean? Okay? What does that mean, Leland? Mom is worried about you. You need to find a girlfriend."

"I don't know if she's my type."

"How are you going to know if you don't give her a chance? Look at me. I didn't know I was going to fall for Gabby the way I have."

"What are they saying?" Gabriella whispered loudly in my ear from behind.

"Leland isn't sure I'm his type and Martin said to give me a chance because he didn't know you were perfect for him until he gave you a chance."

"Really? Marty really said that?" I could hear the emotion in her voice and I grinned. At least Gabriella had found someone worthwhile.

"You can't tell me she's not pretty enough," Martin continued.

"Oh, she's beautiful. It's just..."

"Just what, Leland?" Martin had a perturbed look on his face as he tossed his napkin onto the table.

"You just don't understand." Leland stood from the table and made his way our direction.

"Here he comes," I said. "We better get into the bathroom." I grabbed Gabriella by the arm and pulled her into the room.

"Did they say anything else?" She questioned me as soon as I pushed the door shut.

"Leland is firm about me not being his type and Martin got a little upset with him. I'm not sure we should have eaves dropped on their conversation." I felt a little guilty.

"Why not? It's good to know. When we go dancing don't feel bad about checking out other guys," she said indifferently as she looked at herself in the mirror and smoothed out her makeup.

Leland still hadn't returned to the table when Gabriella and I took our seats once again. We waited a few minutes before Martin said he was going to go see what was holding Leland up. He stood from the table and started making his way toward the latticed area when Leland appeared from around the corner. It almost looked as if he'd been crying.

When the two returned Martin said, "Shall we?" They both held our chairs and escorted us to the limo. Leland was more open in the limo on the ride to the club and he and I had a real conversation about the hotel his family owned.

When we reached the club Martin ordered a bottle of wine for us and immediately swept Gabriella out onto the dance floor. I watched them dance for a couple of songs while taking in the rest of the establishment making sure to glance at Leland from time to time.

He finally noticed my sideward glances and began to talk. "Gabriella thinks Martin spends big bucks on her but really, we get our meals for free so he can afford to buy her the roses and the limo belongs to the hotel too. Well, it does belong to us but if we had a client that needed to be picked up at the airport or driven anywhere else, the limo wouldn't be available. Customers first, you know."

"That's what makes a good business," I supported him.

"Exactly." The conversation ended there and we both let our eyes wander back to Martin and Gabriella on the dance floor.

Finally a slow song began and I felt like I was intruding on a private moment so I let my eyes wander. I picked out a few good looking men that I wouldn't mind flirting with but I didn't want to do that to Leland, no matter what Gabriella said. He didn't have enough self-esteem and didn't need me adding to his complex. My eyes flitted to him to see if he was showing any interest and my own self-esteem started to drop until I followed his gaze. He was watching the same men I was.

"He's cute, don't you think?" I took a chance at damaging his ego.

Leland slowly looked at me with horror in his eyes. "What?"

"Well, I don't want to be rude, but you seem to be staring at that man over there. The dark haired guy?"

"Oh, I hadn't even seen him yet." He was clearly taken with the man's good looks enough to let his guard drop. He pulled away from me and asked, "How did you…"

"I guessed. You seemed to be checking out the same faces in the crowd that I was and I haven't really noticed any of the women in the place yet," I lied. I'd already tried to memorize every face in the building.

"Martin doesn't know," he said quickly. "Well, I think he suspects and doesn't approve."

I reached over to refill Leland's glass and noticed he'd already drank the entire bottle except for the glass that sat in front of me. I called the waitress over and told Leland I would buy this round.

We each ordered something more substantial and sat quietly until they arrived. I, of course, had a shot of whiskey and Leland had ordered two shots of scotch. We clinked our glasses together and downed our shots and Leland immediately picked up his second scotch and swigged that down too.

Gabriella and Martin had found a different table and left Leland and I alone. We ordered more drinks but I made sure to order cola only. I didn't need to get all messed up on a fake date.

Suddenly Leland started to pour out his life story. Great, I thought, but he made it short and to the point. He'd preferred men for as long as he could remember but his mother had harped on him and Martin about carrying on their father's name so often and early enough that he'd never told anyone of his preference.

"I'm sorry," he slurred. "I shouldn't be dumping this on you. I really shouldn't drink either." He let out a small burp.

"No, it's okay," I forgave him.

The two of us started to openly admire the men in the joint and guessing about their lives.

"I bet he's a... dog groomer," I spit out, pointing out a man to Leland. He started to laugh at my guess and so did I. I didn't intend to spend my night trying to cheer up my date and acting silly to do it, but it wasn't all that bad. At the end of the night I felt as if I'd done something good, even if I hadn't helped him at all.

Leland and Martin dropped us off at Gabriella's house. Gabriella couldn't wait to get me inside so she could ask about how we seemed to hit it off at the club.

"You two seemed to warm up to each other after we left you alone at the club."

"Yeah. I made a new friend," I smiled at her.

"Wasn't there any chemistry there?" She was disappointed.

"I wasn't attracted to him and he most definitely wasn't attracted to me." I was still smiling.

"Alex, you have to get past White for a while. Who knows, you might find someone you like better. Plus how could he NOT be attracted to you with that dress on?"

I didn't say anything but gave her a sly look until she finally caught on.

"No!"

"Yes. But don't tell Martin. He's not told him or their mother."

"No way am I telling Martin!" She smiled back at me. We talked about the evening until we both started yawning.

Gabriella rose from the couch, stretching. "You can stay the night here if you want. I'm sorry but I can't drive you home. I've had too much to drink."

"Thanks Gabriella but I'll take a cab. I don't mind."

She flopped back down on the couch to keep me company until my ride arrived.

"I'm sorry your date sucked," she said when the cab pulled into the driveway.

"Not your fault," I laughed.

"Don't you dare tell White that Leland wasn't the perfect gentleman," she warned.

"I won't."

The cab ride was peaceful and I was glad the night was over. I walked slowly into the building, greeted security and took the elevator to the roof. I'd gotten used to being outside under the stars over the past few months and wasn't ready to go to bed yet.

I reached the roof and stepped out into the cool night air and gave a little shiver. Though I was chilly, I welcomed the breeze through my hair. It had a cleansing quality to it.

"You're home early," I heard White's voice from behind me.

I was startled but turned slowly toward his voice. "Not really. It's after midnight."

"But the clubs are still open."

"Gabriella had her fill I guess," I shrugged.

"So, how was the date?" he asked casually.

"Well, we ate at the Maddison. Martin and Leland own it, you know." I went on to explain our meal and then simply stated, "Then we went dancing."

"Sounds like," he smiled, "fun."

"Yeah, it was nice," I managed a satisfied sigh.

This made him look closer at me but his smile returned, even bigger than before.

"What?"

"It was a flop. Wasn't it?"

"No, it was nice," I tried to convince him.

"I can tell you're lying, Alex." One eyebrow raised in amusement.

I couldn't help it and I started to laugh. "Okay. Don't tell Gabriella I told you but Leland turned out to be gay." I wanted to make White jealous but had always been a bad liar. As it turned out it was even harder for me to lie to White.

"Really?" His smile practically split his face in two.

"Knock it off," I gave him a soft push.

"Or what?" He pushed me back.

"Don't push me," I feigned anger.

"Or what?" he asked again backing me into a corner.

My legs began to shake as I struggled to come up with something else.

"Here," he took off his jacket and wrapped it around my shoulders. "You're shivering."

"Thank you," the playfulness died down and we walked to the best spot on the roof. The view of the city was beautiful and we sat in silence for a long time before I gave White his jacket back.

"Thanks. I better get home. Black will be there to get me in only a few hours."

"I'll ride down with you."

When we reached my floor I reminded him not to say a word to Gabriella or I would figure out something to get even and left him to ride down to his apartment alone.

# Chapter Five

I spent the next week sweating it up with Black at the gym and getting huge reading assignments from Red. Every day, after my training with Red, I stopped into White's office in hopes of hearing something more about Dimitri and Grigori. It wasn't just curiosity that kept me interested it was that the job felt unfinished.

At the end of the week White told me he knew I was fishing for more information but that he wasn't privy to all the government's secrets. Then he changed the subject to our Alaskan trip.

"We need to leave early in the morning. It's a long flight so make sure to get plenty of sleep tonight."

I hadn't packed yet so I left his office to do just that.

When I got back to my apartment I did a little more research into the Alaskan compound to help me decide what to bring along. I was packed and ready to go fifteen minutes later. Soon I found myself pacing around in my apartment and made myself find something to do.

The government database was just a few pokes on my keyboard away so I started poking. I was intrigued that Dimitri could fake his death and get away with it for more than two years.

Either Colin hadn't told anyone about our discovery or they hadn't updated their information yet because I didn't find anything more than what I'd read when I'd done my research for The Rave job. I resolved to come back to this again and went to bed.

I awoke to the sound of my telephone ringing. Jumping out of bed I ran to the phone and was greeted with Whites voice. "Are you ready?"

"Yes, but isn't it a little early?" I had glanced at my alarm clock as I dashed to answer the phone and it was only 1:43 AM.

"Not if we want to catch our flight. Meet me at the office right away." He didn't even say good-bye.

My heart was racing from the unexpected phone call and my hands shook as I grabbed my bag and laptop. I was out the door in less than two minutes. He was just locking up the office as I stepped onto the seventh floor.

"Hold the elevator. I'm coming."

I quickly stuck my hand in front of the doors. They jerked fully open again. White picked up his bag, joined me in the elevator and pushed the button for the lobby.

As we walked to White's jet-black mustang he told me our flight left in about an hour.

"Why don't we just fly there ourselves?" I asked.

"The chopper is too slow and it's several hours out of our way to get to any of our planes around here. It'll be faster to take a commercial flight to Fairbanks and then have our guys pick us up there. It's also cheaper to buy a ticket and let the airline pay for the fuel."

We rode the majority of the way to the airport in silence, but when we were within sight of the facility White said, "Our seats aren't together on the flight out. I saved a little money by taking what they had left over."

I nodded my understanding and he continued, "Can you reach back in my bag and get our tickets?"

"Yeah," I removed my seat belt and twisted toward the back seat. "Where are they?" I asked, searching the side pockets.

"They're in the main body of the pack. I think I threw them in first so you're going to have to dig."

"Figures," I mumbled under my breath.

"What?"

"I said, 'Figures.'"

"You think I did it on purpose?"

"Anyone with a brain wouldn't put the tickets in first. It's the first thing you are going to need from your pack. You should know better than that." I was slightly perturbed. He really should know better than this. When Black and I were at the cabin the first time, he talked to me about packing correctly, making sure everything was easily accessible, especially if you might need an item immediately. I turned slightly to glare at White and noticed he wasn't watching the road, his eyes were trained on my seat and I don't mean my car seat. I was instantly embarrassed and angry at the same time. He must have planned it! I flipped around and quickly sat back down, jamming my seat belt back in its place.

"If you don't know how to pack then you can find them."

"But we need to show them before they will let us on airport property." He didn't know I had busted him. Months ago we almost shared a moment but it was cut short by an unexpected visit from Black. Our "almost" moment led to a discussion about our mutual attraction and that led to White being the gentleman and suggesting we become friends. We'd definitely become closer over the past few months but I had almost resigned myself to being friends only. I was afraid to make myself available to him anyway. This was the first time White had shown any risqué behavior since then. I wondered if it had anything to do with my recent date.

"I don't care. You can get them yourself. I refuse to dig through your pack for tickets you knew we were going to need." We sat quietly after that but my mind was racing. I was embarrassed and upset, but there were other emotions mixed in with the other two. I was flattered that he would go to that much trouble just for a look but I would never let him know that. I guess I liked the attention but didn't want to admit it, not even to myself. I also knew if it had been any other man I would have felt violated, but that feeling was strangely absent. I felt my face begin to flush and quickly calmed myself down. I glanced in Whites direction and he was faithfully watching the road with a half grin on his face. His smile made me realize I wore a stupid grin myself. It took some doing but I forced myself to put it away. Maybe he thought we were good enough friends now. I wasn't convinced yet.

When we reached the airport security guard shack, White had to get out and dig through his bag, but he knew exactly where the tickets were so it didn't take him as long as I had hoped. He showed the guards and we were granted access after they searched the trunk.

"I hope we aren't late because of that." He tried to make me feel guilty for not finding them.

"Dang it, me too." I feigned concern and rolled my eyes. He paid a daily parking fee and told me the partners would come retrieve his car later and we walked into the building.

I'd flown in company, private or military aircraft, but the experience of flying on a commercial flight was new to me. The security at the airport was thick and demanding, but I expected more. If a person really wanted or needed to get something past airport security there were several ways to do it. It made the thought of the long flight ahead of me a little unnerving.

Eventually we made our way to the plane and boarded. White was a few seats ahead of me in the aisle. I, on the other hand, had a window seat. I wasn't able to see White without standing and that made me a little uncomfortable. I felt like I was traveling alone.

The first leg of the trip I spent my time staring out the window. There's nothing like seeing the earth grow further from your feet. It fascinated me every time, especially in the dark. When we came in for our landing I became restless and found myself standing as soon as we came to a stop. White was still in his seat and I felt a little more at ease. He started to turn my direction so I sat down quickly and waited for others to stand before I stood again. We made our connection without hassle or delay and we were off once more. We repeated this motion twice more before we reached Fairbanks.

The air was noticeably cooler, but not as cold as I had anticipated. "This isn't as bad as I thought it would be," I related to White as we crossed into the airport.

"We aren't done yet," was all that he said as he led me over to a man sitting in a chair waiting for us. He was of average build with a full beard but a younger face under all that coarse hair.

"Sam," White greeted the man as he stood and shook White's hand. I knew he was one of the men I'd selected for my teams.

"Good to see you again, sir." Sam looked toward me.

"This is Commander Grey," White introduced me.

Sam quickly saluted me and then thrust his hand out for me to shake. I took it and said, "Good to meet you, Sam."

"Well, I'm ready whenever you two are." The tone had gone from formal to very informal in a matter of seconds.

"Lets get going then." White instructed.

We boarded the small plane and began the last leg of our journey. White and I had already been in the air more than ten hours and we still had at least an hour left. I contemplated napping for the short flight to where ever it was we were going to end up but I couldn't tear myself from the window. The view was so spectacular. The mountains, water, snow and desolation all worked well together. It conjured up images from Jack London stories I had read and then some of it reminded me of shows on the National Geographic channel but, whatever thought it brought to mind, it brought the feel of adventure. To get lost out here would be a challenge that not many people would be able to conquer. The time went by so fast I was disappointed when White said, "There's the compound," and pointed off to our right.

The compound was on the edge of a huge lake that looked like a gash in the earth. I had seen many lakes from the air during our flight, but the lakes closer to the compound looked unnatural. They all looked like some kind of open wound on the face of the earth. I could picture the Loch Ness monster raising her head above the surface of each and every one of them and was apprehensive when we landed on the water itself.

White stepped out of the plane onto the dock and stuck his hand out toward me. I almost took it for help down to the dock, but at the last second I handed him his bag. I picked mine up and turned back to find White's hand had returned so I handed him my bag as well. He quickly tossed it aside and offered his hand once more. I graciously took it and stepped from the plane.

Sam took both of our bags and walked away from the waters edge. He turned back to us just long enough to say, "I'll take your bags to your barracks, sir."

White thanked him and said to me, "Come on, I'll show you around." He led me away from the water and toward the many buildings several yards away. After choosing this compound I had studied the satellite pictures thoroughly and thought I would know the place well when I got here, but that was not the case. Looking down from the sky and actually walking between the buildings are two different things. The compound was much larger than I expected, considering there were only thirty-two people stationed here.

The first building we came to was the compound Headquarters. White explained that the building held it's very own C.I.C. and library and, of course, it was the most important building on the entire compound. We didn't go in, but moved off to the southeast to a building about a third of the size of Headquarters.

"This is the Iceberg Lounge," White said as we stepped inside.

"Straight to the bar?" I gave him a disapproving look, although a quick shot of something was tempting. Just to get warmed up. However, I told myself, that doesn't really warm you up. I know, but my nerves are frazzled, I continued to talk to myself internally. I decided to wait to see what White was up to.

"This is Joe," White introduced me to the bartender. He was an Alaskan Indian in his late 50's. I reached out and shook his hand. White introduced me as Commander Grey.

"Nice to meet you Commander. Are you going to be staying with us long?"

"Just a few days."

"Inspection time again." White made a little more small talk with Joe and then ordered two cups of coffee. Then he led me to a table in the corner.

"I thought a cup of coffee after that long flight would do us both some good."

I agreed with him and then he continued to explain the compound further. It consisted of two huge hangers, which I could easily see from anywhere on the compound. Hanger A was the aircraft hanger and Hanger B was reserved for the motor pool. The entire compound was self sufficient, producing it's own electricity and hiring local people to run the bar, store and various other tasks, such as general housekeeping. The thing that surprised me the most about the compound was the amount of people it could house comfortably. There were four regular barracks that could house forty men each.

Then the Officer's Barracks had ten rooms available. That's where we would be staying.

My office would be in the building right next to my living quarters and that building also housed the mess hall; which also doubled for a rec. hall when not in use for meals.

White went on to explain to me the men that had spent a good deal of time here could be quite rough around the edges, but I absolutely could not let them get the best of me. He continued to lecture me about management for the better part of fifteen minutes. Then he switched the subject over to the local people who helped run the compound. He warned me against offending them.

"The smooth operation of our facilities depends mainly on our local help."

"Understood. However, I have no intentions of offending anyone."

"Our cadets go through an orientation with every compound they visit, so consider this your orientation." Men started to trickle in slowly as we talked and each of them greeted White with "Commander" and me with a variety of looks from stunned to intrigued. We talked for another half an hour and several cups of coffee. Finally we said good-bye to Joe and made our way to the Officer's Barracks. I noticed at least a 30° temperature difference as we stepped from the Iceberg and then again when we walked into the barracks. It took a little while for me to warm back up.

While I tried to control my shivering, White showed me around the Officer's Barracks. It was a two-story building with a front lobby and a guard on each floor. My room, on the second floor, was right next to White's and looked like a suite in a fancy hotel. It contained a sitting room with a television, a bedroom, a little kitchenette with a table that seated four and a bathroom. There was one window in the sitting room that was curtained with dark, heavy drapes. White left me to unpack and said he'd be back in an hour to collect me for dinner.

I still hadn't warmed up so I took a hot shower. It helped warm me up immediately and was welcome refreshment after our long trip. I pulled my hair back into a braid, set up my laptop on the small desk near the television and killed time while I waited for White.

He arrived in an hour, as promised, and we walked the short distance to the mess hall. There were only five tables set up in the large area and the men seated at them were all visiting quietly until they noticed White and me. Then they stood and saluted White who saluted back. None of them had food in front of them yet, but they sat back down and resumed talking in subdued tones. We continued walking past them toward a hallway in the back of the mess hall. White pointed out all the rooms and their functions. First was the mess hall/rec hall we had already passed through and as we entered the hallway White pointed out the kitchen doorway. Inside were three women doing various things to prepare the dinner. One of the younger ladies looked up and saw White. She stood up straight and gazed at him with obvious awe, until she saw me, then she adverted her eyes quickly and went back to her duties. I looked at White questioningly and he avoided the look. This made me wonder about his relationship with this girl. Was there a relationship there, or had there been?

As we continued our walk down the hallway White pointed out two offices on our right and two classrooms on the left. "I'm not sure which one we are going to put you in yet. I need to talk to Johns and ask him which one isn't being utilized."

"Johns?" I hadn't met a Johns yet.

"He's the commanding officer of this compound. We'll sit with him at dinner tonight and discuss it." White finished showing me around the building and we made our way back to the mess hall where we got in line for our dinner. After our cafeteria plates were full we took a seat at a table that contained only two other men. Sam was one of them and the other was Johns, the man in charge of the place.

I was introduced and we got right down to business. I was to have the office closest to the mess hall. White said he'd set me up with a password so I could access the computer. Then the talk of business ended and the conversation became more relaxed.

Johns was enthralled with the fact I had no military training and asked me all kinds of questions about it. I told him I trained under Master Chief Slade and he was surprised at that as well. The questioning continued until White started answering for me. This irritated me somewhat but I was too tired to argue. Soon after White took to answering Johns' questions I glanced at my watch. It was after 10 o'clock. I had been stifling a yawn for some time now so I took my leave.

I rose from the table and so did the three men. I smiled my appreciation at them. It was nice to be acknowledged as a woman from time to time. I noticed a few men scattered around at different tables as I walked toward the door. I don't know why, but when I reached the door I turned around and looked back into the room. All eyes were on me and some of the men had joined White, Johns and Sam at our table. Immediately a nervous feeling started boiling in my stomach. I quickly turned around and stepped outside. It was full daylight and it startled me. I checked my watch again and as I did this my brain reminded me where I was and I got a flash of the heavy drapes in my room.

I made my way back to my room and immediately got into bed. It had been a long day and I knew tomorrow would be hectic as well. I was tired but couldn't make my mind slow down long enough to fall asleep. I knew I was the talk of the place. First and foremost, I was a woman in a place with not much diversity in that subject. Not that there was anything wrong with the women already on the compound. Secondly, I outranked everyone here, except White. Even the CO of the compound, Johns, had to answer to me if I demanded it. Then to top it all off, the thought of White stealing a glance at my backside had me in knots. I knew I'd like to be involved with him, at least in my fantasy world. The real world was a lot more complicated though and I still wasn't quite ready for it. Black saved me once from having to make a decision I wasn't ready for. I only hoped he'd be around *this* time.

Despite my overactive thoughts I fell asleep and awoke with a start. I was confused for a split second until I remembered where I was. My stomach did a flip and I got myself out of bed and started my morning routine. I had barely dried off from my shower when White showed up at my door.

"Do you have coffee made?" He lifted a coffee cup for me to see.

"Yes," I let him in. He walked right to the kitchenette area and poured himself a cup.

"You're coffee is better than Joe's. Plus, he won't be open today and neither is the kitchen." He took a seat in one of the chairs at the table. I refreshed my own cup and sat across from him.

He sipped his coffee for a few minutes then said, "I've got some things to do so we won't see much of each other today. If you need anything you can ask Cadet Sullivan at Headquarters." We sat quietly after that until White finished his coffee. Then he got up, filled his cup again, said thanks and left me alone. I allowed myself one more cup of coffee before I took a run around the compound.

I walked out of the Officers barracks' east entrance and got a beautiful view of the lake. It was bitingly cold and I knew I would have to fight against shivering until I got my blood pumping through my veins. Black had reminded me of how much I actually enjoyed my morning workouts, in whatever form they came. I took the opportunity to try to become more familiar with the compound from the ground.

The path I took led me along the edge of the lake. When we'd been in the air it looked as if it were a gash in the earth with no bottom. From this vantage point the water was pristine and I could clearly follow the rocky bottom until it dropped off sharply. At that point, the water changed from clear to an inky black. I ran past the dock where the plane we arrived in was moored and then on past the boathouse all the way to the utility building where the road ended in a cul-de-sac. I longed to keep following the lake but doubled back to the boathouse and turned to the west. I soon found my way to the Iceberg Lounge. I glanced at my watch and more time had passed than I had expected so I turned to go back to my room.

When I walked inside I realized I hadn't seen anyone else out and about. The compound was quiet. I found this unusual for a training compound. I pictured a place where the men would be forced out of bed at the crack of dawn by a yelling drill instructor. White had told me they stuck pretty close to military standards but I didn't see that here.

I took another shower and reminded myself if I planned on running in the mornings, I might as well wait to shower until after I got back. Not only because I didn't need two showers every morning but also because my wet hair was almost frozen from my outing.

This time I left the building by the west entrance and crossed the street to the mess hall. I expected to see men seated at their tables, eating breakfast, but the building was empty. Even the kitchen was uninhabited. Then I remembered White saying the kitchen wouldn't be open today. Must be because it's Sunday.

I opened my laptop and connected to the network using White's password for C.I.C. in his apartment. I was a little surprised he used the same password. I had already read about the men stationed here but realized I didn't bring hard copies of their records. Instead, I went in search of a printer and found one at Headquarters. Cadet Sullivan pointed me in the right direction without a word. When I returned to my room I double-checked everything. All was in order and I had time to kill. I was hungry and starting to feel sorry for myself so I decided to take a walk to the store. Maybe everything didn't close on Sunday.

It was still quiet and I began to wonder where everyone was. The store was across the street to the south of my barracks so I didn't have far to go. I stepped up the three stairs to the door and it was locked. I headed back to my room to pout but decided against it. I was going to do some more wandering.

In less than an hour I had been to every building on the compound, minus the men's barracks. There wasn't a soul to be found except the one cadet in Headquarters. I dreaded it, but I decided to walk toward the barracks. This quiet was really beginning to bother me. I liked the peace, but quiet in a place like this was too weird. I felt like I was stranded in a ghost town. When I reached the barracks I walked a little slower, hoping to hear sounds of life inside, but there were none. I wanted to go to a door and knock but decided against it. I couldn't think of a good excuse as to why I would be there. I could tell the truth, but then they might think I was a big baby. Nope, I'll just go back to my room.

I watched TV for a while but kept the volume low so I could hear any noises that might occur outside, or next door. After an hour or so I got up and went to White's room. I had been putting it off because he told me he had things to do today and I didn't want to bother him but I couldn't stand much more of this.

I knocked and received no answer. Strange things began to go through my mind. Was this another test? Did I need to find my way back to civilization or try to survive for so many days out here, all alone? But I'm not all alone, I reminded myself. I hiked to Headquarters and cornered the poor cadet at the desk. I hadn't really looked at him before but this time I noticed he was close to my age, maybe a year or two older. He wasn't a bad looking man either. Being stranded up here with a man like this might not be all that bad, I guess. I giggled inwardly for only a second then the reality of being stranded up here hit me.

"Where is everybody?" I asked him, successfully suppressing my anxiety.

"Sunday operations." He looked at me like I was crazy. Maybe I didn't suppress my concern as well as I thought.

"Oh, I see. How long will they be gone?"

"Until they get back." I didn't like his tone. He was treating me as if I were an idiot.

"Really?" I was irritated. "What time do you expect them back, cadet?" I changed my tone from conversational to commanding.

"Usually around twenty-two hundred hours, Ma'am." He'd gotten the hint but there was disdain in the word Ma'am.

I wanted to say more, but was flabbergasted by his attitude. I turned to leave and I heard Sullivan mutter something under his breath that sounded a lot like, "Stupid bitch." I quickly turned around and asked, "Did you have something more to say, cadet?"

"No, Ma'am." Again, the Ma'am was full of scorn.

I gave him a dirty look and turned to leave again and again he muttered something under his breath but this time I was sure of what I heard and it was horribly offensive. I stopped, turned and said, "This is unacceptable, Sullivan. I don't care for your attitude and I won't put up with it. I demand an apology right now." I pointed my finger at the ground in emphasis. In answer to my demand Sullivan rolled his eyes and shook his head.

"I don't think you realize what kind of a mistake you are making, cadet," I said when he wouldn't comply.

"Is that so? You are here for inspections, big deal. I'm not worried." He suddenly became distracted by a fingernail on his left hand and refused to look up. I stood in a state of semi-shock for a few seconds then I straightened my spine. Who was this punk? I had the authority to send him packing and I'd make sure he knew that.

"Stand at attention, cadet." I ordered but he only stuck the fingernail he'd been considering in his mouth and began to gnaw. "I am going to give you the benefit of the doubt and explain something to you. When my explanation is complete you will obey the order or be dismissed from your duties as soon as Commander White returns."

This got his attention, but not in the way I wanted. "I knew it. You are his new pet and you think that'll get me fired. Let me tell you something, sweetie. White loves his company more than *any* woman and won't take your side on this."

"You'd do better to open your ears and shut your mouth, Sullivan. I am the newest partner. I have as much pull as White and he will back me up before he even hears your side of the story. I *do* have the authority to terminate your employment with this company for no better reason than I'm having a bad day. I suggest you put a stopper in the attitude, stand at attention and apologize."

"I will not take orders from a snooping, skinny, stupid woman."

"We shall see," I replied and walked from the building. All the way back to my barracks I thought of ways I could have decked him. When I got into my room I made myself find things to occupy my time while I waited for White to return. I wanted to tell him about Sullivan, but I didn't want to admit that he was right about coming here to baby-sit me. I kept going over the scene in my head and finally came to the conclusion that it wasn't my fault. I had done nothing to deserve the disrespect Sullivan had shown. Even if the tables had been turned and he had been the ranking officer, he still would have been wrong to act the way he did.

I dozed off on the loveseat while I waited and woke to a knock at my door. It was White so I let him in. He told me about his day. All of the men, except Sullivan and White, left the night before and hiked into the wilderness where they had to run some cold weather drills, such as taking their guns apart and putting them back together in the cold. White explained how hard it was to do that with numb fingers. He went into more detail but I didn't really listen. I was struggling to decide how I should tell him about Sullivan's attitude.

Eventually White noticed I didn't have much to say besides, "Yeah" and "Uh, huh."

"So, how did your day go?" He said with apprehension.

"Not bad. I didn't know where everyone went though. I almost started hiking myself. I thought this might be another test to see if I could get out of the Alaskan wilderness alone."

"Are you mad at me because I didn't tell you where I was going?" His voice became amused.

"No." He thought I was being possessive.

"Well, what then? You're too quiet."

"I assume the men normally have a daily exercise routine?"

"Yes. Why?"

"I'd like to lead them in the morning if that's all right."

"I'm sure we can work that out. Why?" He asked again, his expression grim.

"I think I should use Black's tactics. You were right. I need to make the men respect me." I shrugged.

"What happened?" His tone became ominous and I began to regret even mentioning it.

I started to tell him the story and when I reached the part where Sullivan called me names White jumped up and yelled, "What?" He was half way to the door by the time I caught his arm.

"Let me finish. I threatened his job," White cut me off in mid sentence.

"As you should have. As far as I'm concerned, Sullivan no longer works with the company."

"I don't know if I want to go that far yet. Lets give him a little time to consider what he's done. His attitude doesn't make sense. I'm not sure he's rational." I didn't understand my feelings of guilt in this matter, but they were there all the same.

"I'm sorry, Alex, but I don't agree. We can't afford this type of attitude in the company." He pulled his arm free and grabbed his coat. My objections went unheard as he left my room. I put my coat on and followed after him before I realized I didn't have my shoes on. I went back into my room and slipped them on. I didn't even take the time to tie them. White was already gone and I didn't catch up to him until right outside Headquarters.

"White," I started to say but he ignored me and went inside so I followed, right on his heels.

Cadet Sullivan had company and they all jumped to their feet and stood at attention as White and I stormed in. "Commander White," Sullivan said and the other two men backed away from him somewhat.

"I've just been told some very disturbing news, Sullivan." White's voice was dripping with rage.

"What would that be, sir?" Sullivan feigned innocence.

"We both know what I'm talking about. Commander Grey informed me of your termination and I wanted you to know it is official. I will draw up your last check and have Sam fly you to the nearest airport as soon as he can find time."

"What?" Now Sullivan was grasping it. I felt a surge of glee followed by those same feelings of guilt. I knew Sullivan had been wrong, but I didn't want to be the reason a man lost his job.

"You are relieved of your duties as of now. I suggest you get your stuff together." White's tone remained terse and stern and it put me on edge.

Sullivan diverted his attention to me and yelled, "You got me fired, you stupid bitch!"

I knew what was coming before I ever saw him move so I was between White and Sullivan before White could connect with his punch. I grabbed White's arm and slowed him enough so Sullivan could dodge out of the way.

"No." I said calmly and White got a hold of himself.

"I knew you were his whore!" Sullivan said from behind me. I kept Whites gaze until I was sure he wouldn't try to go after Sullivan again then I turned around.

"Sullivan, you are walking on thin ice here. I actually didn't want to fire you but now I've changed my mind. You may go now." I added this last part just to make him mad and it worked. He lunged for me and I was aware of White moving in to intercept but I was faster than both of them. I got in a good punch to Sullivan's eye and had him down on his knees before either he or White could get involved in the fight.

"Nice," White complimented me.

"Thanks," I said as I held Sullivan's arm stretched straight out behind him. Black had put me in this position a time or two and it was very uncomfortable. If a person struggled too much they would break their own arm. Sullivan sat stiffly on his knees trying to catch his breath. He didn't say anything more so I knew he had his anger under control. This meant one of two things. He could be coming up with a plan or he had conceded. I decided to find out which one it was and released him. He pulled his arm around and clutched it to his body. I had made a perfect shot to his eye and it was beginning to redden. He looked at White and started to say something but White shook his head ominously.

"Take him into custody, gentlemen," he told the other two.

Other than a wild look and tense body language, Sullivan didn't protest any further and allowed the two cadets to lead him away.

When the two cadets returned they immediately saluted White who said, "At ease. Were you two here to relieve Sullivan?"

"Yes, sir," they both answered him.

"Carry on then." White turned to face me and said, "Shall we?" Then we both moved toward the door. On the way back to the Officer's barracks White said he should inform Johns of the incident and I should come with him. We went directly to Johns' room and were greeted warmly. Once inside, I could tell the room was well lived in. My room was more like a hotel room, but Johns had his set up more like an apartment with many personal things throughout. He had pictures hung on the walls, a computer desk with a printer but no computer and other personal belongings and all had the look of permanence.

White and I took a seat at the small table in the kitchenette area and Johns said, "So, what brings you two here at this time of night?"

"I fired one of your guys." White informed him.

"Who?" Johns asked.

"Sullivan."

"Sullivan?" Johns' voice was troubled. "What happened?"

"He is disrespectful and combative," White was still tense.

"I'll take care of it immediately." Johns started to make moves to leave.

"I've already taken care of it. He's in custody and I'll have Sam fly him out of here tomorrow. " White made it clear this was final by changing the subject.

"What time do the men usually get up for morning drills?"

"We've cut it down to just Sunday drills," Johns said guiltily.

"Is that so? Johns, I have to say what I'm finding up here is a disaster so far. We'll begin at," he looked at me.

"Four A.M." I answered him.

"Understood."

"We better all get some sleep so we'll be ready for the long day tomorrow." White added and turned to go.

I followed him out of the room and as soon as the door was shut behind us I said, "Is this normal?"

"No. Johns is officially up for review and I've decided I'm going to demote him. This is unacceptable from someone we've promoted to CO." White was angry. He didn't allow me to reply and left me standing outside my room alone. It was going to be a long day tomorrow and I needed to get some sleep. The one thing I wouldn't do is stand on the sidelines and bark orders. I planned on showing these men I could outdo them.

# Chapter Six

White must have still been in bed when I knocked on his door the next morning because he answered in nothing but a pair of pajama pants, catching me off guard. He noticed my reaction and grinned at me.

"Excuse me, I'll get dressed." He was clearly amused which embarrassed me further. My face became hot and I avoided looking at him until he turned away from me but then I took one more look. It was for the best, I told myself. He shouldn't be answering the door like that anyway.

He emerged from his bedroom fully dressed and said, "Is this better?" My face started to feel hot again but I shrugged it off and changed the subject.

"How exactly do you want to do this?"

"*You* are going to go get them out of bed. We are only utilizing one of the barracks right now, so that'll make it easier for you." He went onto tell me how to go about rousting the men out of bed. I was to be loud, direct and demanding. This should be easy enough, I thought.

When we reached the barracks I got a mental picture of White standing in front of me with hardly anything on and became flustered. I did not want to repeat that experience with a different man and especially not with thirty-two different men. I had slowed somewhat and entered behind White. The building wasn't set up as I had expected it to be. I'd envisioned one large room with men in beds in a row along each wall, but this was much more private. We were standing in a long hallway with doors on each side of us for the length of the hall and one door at the other end.

"There are twenty rooms and we bunk the men two to a room. Just pound on the doors and yell at them to get up."

This might be easier than I thought. I began on one side of the hall and started banging my fists on the doors and yelling, "Up and at 'em boys. Let's go," and other similar phrases. Some of the men were already coming out of their rooms when I reached the end of the hall and started making my way back down the line of doors on the other side. Most of them had confused looks on their faces but they all stood at attention including White at the far end of the hall. Soon the entire barracks were standing at attention outside their doors. White took the liberty of addressing the men at that point. He introduced me and explained to them I was going to head the morning drills. Then he spoke to me quietly.

"I'll go get Johns and meet you at the open area across from Headquarters." Then he left me alone with the men.

When all the men stopped exiting their rooms I said in a commanding voice, "Out!" I'd learned a few one word commands from Black.

I instructed the men to line up once we were outside. As soon as they were in formation I led my troop on a nice little run to the open field where I was to meet White and Johns. They weren't there when we reached it so we began our pushups without them. We started with fifty and by pushup forty-eight White and Johns showed up. I led them in a fast run around the open field. After the third lap around, White and I were the only ones not out of breath. I slowed our pace to a jog for the next two laps and some of the men were able to catch their breath but Johns dropped out.

As we lapped him I said, "Only four more laps Commander." I heard some of the men groan behind me so I threw back at them, "unless I lose count." I didn't hear any more complaints and everyone kept up. As we finished our last lap I led at a slow jog to the mess hall. Once we stopped I turned around to see the men walking around or standing doubled over trying to get their breath back. I will admit, I had given myself a good workout and White was a little sweaty and breathless. He gave me a huge grin when I looked at him. I didn't return it for fear of the men seeing it. I let them mill around for a little while and then called them to attention again. They lined up as expected and I marched them into the mess hall. Breakfast was still being prepared so I let the men take a breather before they ate. I went to my office and White followed me.

"Good workout," he complimented me as he shut the door to the room.

"But bad timing. I didn't really want to give them much of a break before breakfast." I would get it down eventually.

"Well, think of it this way; at least they'll be able to hold their breakfast down now that they've had a bit of a rest." He winked at me.

"I didn't think they'd be this badly out of shape." I commented as I started laying out paperwork on the desk.

"Me either. This is going to be good for them. I'm really disappointed in Johns. He should be doing more than just Sunday drills."

"Yep, and he should march with the men too, no more driving along side of them." I added.

"I'm not going to tell him he's demoted until I have someone lined up to come replace him though. We really should get to the compounds more often than we do. We obviously need to keep a better eye on things, at least here." White admitted.

I mentioned Sullivan and White said he'd round him up after breakfast.

I looked at White As we sat down to eat and was going to make conversation, but he shook his head and put his fingers to his lips. I thought this was strange until I noticed the entire room was devoid of conversation. This must be standard procedure, I thought. The only sounds were utensils on plates and the women in the kitchen. I ate as fast as I could and when I got up to go to my office all the men rose, whether they were done eating or not. I emptied my left over food into the trash with a line of men behind me, waiting to do the same. One by one they lined up at attention. They stood in rigid formation for a time before White curtly dismissed them. He left me alone in my office, saying he'd be back after he'd given Sam the responsibility of getting rid of Sullivan.

About midmorning White returned. He'd let Sam pick two other cadets to accompany him and Sullivan to the nearest airport. The two cadets and Sam would then be sent to another compound.

"I wanted to interview Sam," I groused.

"Sorry, but he was the best choice."

We decided to put off the interviews for a day or two. The men didn't know exactly why we were here anyway so we didn't throw off anyone's schedule. As if they had any schedule up here. White and I kept the rest of the men busy all day and soon it was time for dinner. The evening meal was different than the breakfast and lunch we had all endured. There was conversation at the tables, though it was subdued. I watched some of the men talk and they knew they would have an equally hard day tomorrow so most of them planned on going directly back to their barracks. A few of them complained about the shrew that came with White and I was glad for it so I would know who to keep a good eye on later. All of this was said quietly but my ability to read lips wasn't common knowledge so I had the advantage.

White was quiet for the duration of the meal but as the men started filing out he asked, "So, what were they saying?"

"They talked about the drills, the early morning start tomorrow and going to bed. Nothing really worth repeating."

"I can remember going through basic and one hot topic was always the drill instructor. I've always wanted to know what the men say about me. Didn't they say anything about you?" He asked.

"Yeah, a few of them had a couple of choice things to say, but I'm glad. That means I'm not too easy and it wasn't all of them so I'm not too hard either. Besides, it'll be good to know who thinks what." I replied.

"Exactly. You are going to have to teach me to read lips. I'd love to know how to do that."

"Sometimes you *hear* something you wish you hadn't. But, if you want to learn how to read lips, you should go to Colin. He's so much better at it than I am. I'm getting better, but I still miss a few words here and there."

"We'll see," White said as he rose from the table. I watched him empty his tray and leave the building. I really had no reason to stay there alone, but I didn't want to follow White around so I sat for a few minutes more. The ladies in the kitchen kept looking out at me so I decided it was time for me to go. As I stepped out into the cold air I decided to go to the Iceberg Lounge for a coffee so White wouldn't hear me come back to my room yet.

Upon entering the bar, I noticed ten men scattered throughout. Most of them were gathered around the pool table but a couple of them were at the bar. I took a seat a short distance away from everyone and said my hellos to Joe. I ordered a coffee and he brought it to me right away. I tipped him generously and watched the scene around me.

I started watching their lips to pass the time more than out of real curiosity of what they were saying. Almost immediately they started talking about me and of course I heard things I really didn't want to. What was it with men and their extreme fascination with the size of particular parts of a woman's anatomy? Was talking about it a male bonding thing, I wondered. To me, it was just stating the obvious. Now, if you were to talk about a hidden tattoo or something unseen by your fellow man that would be worth some conversation. I turned to face into the bar. I had counted the bottles of liquor behind the bar at least twice and decided it was time to go. I didn't fit in here and it was painfully obvious.

I thanked Joe and started for the door when I heard, "Commander Grey." I looked in the direction of the voice and saw a blonde man coming my direction. He had been one of the men with something to say at dinner.

"Yes?" I answered him and noticed the whole place was watching us.

"Jack and Jill over there say you beat the living shit out of Sullivan. I say they are full of it. But the rest of the guys here want to hear your side of the story." Jack and Jill as he called them were the two men that witnessed the confrontation with Sullivan in Headquarters.

"Jack and Jill eh? Well, sounds to me like Jack and Jill are exaggerating a bit. I just reminded Sullivan of his manners." I didn't like this; it could easily turn into a brawl with me in the middle. I kept an eye on every last man in the room as they all came closer. I looked at Joe and he was already on the phone, hopefully calling White to come back me up.

"I didn't say she 'beat the living shit out of Sullivan' I said she stopped Commander White from doing it." It was either Jack or Jill trying to diffuse the situation.

"So, what did Sullivan do to the Commander to piss him off so bad? Did the Commander catch you two in bed?" The blonde man asked me.

"I can tell you've got a couple of drinks under your belt, Cadet. However, I suggest you remember your own manners before you get yourself into the same position Sullivan found himself in." I should have went straight back to my room, I was kicking myself.

If Jack had spoken first then it was Jill who got all the men to divert their attention from me to him. He reenacted the entire scene. He had the blonde man act as White, while Jack was supposed to be Sullivan and Jill became me. I have to admit, he did a good job choreographing the whole thing. It was comical and if that was what it really looked like I can't imagine keeping a straight face watching it from the sidelines. Before the show was over White came in and stood behind me. I was the only one who noticed him enter.

"What's going on?" He asked me quietly.

"Shhhh, watch." I pointed at the show unfolding before us. When it was finished the blonde man turned back to me and informed me he still didn't believe it.

"Good show, Jill. See you in the morning, gentlemen." I said and saw White give them a disapproving look as he and I turned to leave.

"I got a call from Joe saying that you needed my help. What the heck was going on?" White asked as soon as we got outside.

"The blonde guy wanted to start something with me but Jack and Jill stepped in."

"Jack and Jill?"   I could tell he was terribly confused so I started from the beginning.

I finished the story just in time for White to deposit me at my door.


"He had it, almost word for word."   He commented on Jill's show.   "Now, go to bed.   I don't want to have to come bail you out again."

"Don't worry, I will.   Besides, you didn't have to bail me out."

# Chapter Seven

The next morning I didn't hesitate getting the men out of bed and started by banging on White's and Johns' doors first.  Things moved a lot faster when they knew what to expect and all the men were lined up outside their rooms before I reached the end of the hall.  I led everyone in a fast run to the open area we had done the pushups in the previous morning but instead of stopping to do the pushups I led them in five laps instead of ten.  Then I led them directly to the mess hall.  I could tell most of them were relieved that we were going to get a longer break before breakfast this morning.  White asked why I cut the exercise down so much and I told him to have the men set up the mats I'd seen lining the walls.

"I don't want to become monotonous." I explained to him.

We all filed into the building and some of the men were already finding their seats when White hollered at them to set out the mats.  While they were doing that I told White that I wanted to have them spar against each other today because of the incident at the Iceberg last night.  I, especially, wanted a shot at the blonde man who had given me a little trouble.  He agreed and suggested that he and I spar first.

"It won't hurt to give them a show," he added.  I accepted his offer and he was kind enough to explain to the men what we expected of them.  They paired off and started their dances.  White had been sure to save a mat for us and we each took our corner.

He lunged at me and I didn't move fast enough.  In a blink of an eye White had a hold of my arm.  Flipping me to the ground he rolled on top of me as if it were choreographed.

"What are you doing?" He was surprised that he caught me.

"I got distracted," I nodded to our little crowd.

White let me up and we went back at it.  This time I didn't let anything draw my attention away from the hulking beast in front of me. I used to think of White as himself when we sparred and he got the better of me much to often.  Now, I pictured him as not even human. He was a threat.  This helped immensely and the odds of him even touching me during one of our sessions were slim.

"We can't do this all day, so don't be so cautious." I told him.

He tried for me again and I dropped to the floor and did the leg sweep and he was down.

"One to one." I tallied the score for him as we circled each other.

"You haven't done that for a long time," he commented.

This time I went for him first. I came at him like I was going for his middle and as soon as I got within arms reach I turned and found myself behind him. I quickly jumped on his back and had him around the neck. I utilized a pressure point and he fell to his knees. I released him and walked around him to help him up. "Two to one."

"Where did that come from? That's a new one." He reached for my hand and at the last minute he tried to sweep my legs out from under me. He made contact and I started to lose my footing so I gave myself a little push backwards and did a back flip. If White hadn't expected the flip, I would have been able to kick him in the face, but that was one he and I had been working on.

"Now you're just showing off." I said.

He winked at me and then singled out the blonde cadet. "Your turn, Cadet. The rest of you, get to work!"

After our show, Blondie was a little apprehensive about stepping onto the mat but he did make it to his corner. We squared off and he was down on the ground in a matter of seconds. I didn't even have to work for that one.

"Come on," I told him, "make me earn it." I wanted to throw him to the ground a couple of times just to prove a point, but I knew humiliating him wouldn't help matters. I started pointing out technique flaws and showed him a couple of moves before I thanked him and sent him to fight another partner. I ended up sparring with a couple other men and one of them got the better of me. It wouldn't have been all that bad, but he got in a good shot to my shoulder, twice. He hit me in the same exact place both times and it smarted. I couldn't let him know it hurt but I quit my sparring after that and gave up the mat to some of the other men. White and I watched the men fight for an hour and then the women showed up to start cooking breakfast so we called an end to the morning exercises.

I went to my office and White followed me. I wanted to go over more files but White wanted to visit.

"So, what are we going to do tomorrow morning?" He asked.

"I don't know. Probably run laps all morning. I got nailed in the shoulder a couple of times and I think I should let it rest a day or so."

"Do you mind if I take charge tomorrow morning then?" He asked.

"No. I'd actually like that."

"You still haven't trained under me yet, Grey. I don't know if you'll like it. Believe it or not, I'm harder to get along with than Black."

"Black's not hard to get a long with." I corrected him.

"He must have given you a break if you think he's not hard to please. He's too quiet, grouchy and hard to beat in a competition."

"None of that makes him hard to get along with, White." I said. "The quiet is nice. He's never been grouchy with me and I've beat him more than once at different things."

"I suppose you're right. He is a hard ass though, you have to admit that."

"No, I don't. He expects the best you can give but I don't think that makes him a hard ass, just a good teacher." Again, I defended Black.

"Well, if you feel that way about Black then maybe you won't have any problems with my methods," he said.

"I'm going to get some coffee. Do you want some?" I started to get up from my desk.

"No, you finish what you're doing, I'll get it." He left me alone to retrieve my coffee.

I already knew who I wanted to interview but I hadn't talked to White about my picks yet. By sending Sam away, White cut my picks in half. I had some other prospects but they were what White called "grunts" and needed more training than the other men.

When White came back with the coffee I handed him a file.

"Looks like he could be a candidate for Team Grey," he said after he looked it over.

"That's what I thought. I'll put Cadet Stevens in the keeper file."

"Who else have you got?"

"Well, I wanted to interview Sam but you sent him off to who knows where," I complained.

"That couldn't be helped. We'll just have to move onto the next and you can interview Sam later."

"I've got a couple more," I handed him the rest of the files. He flipped through them.

"Is this it?" He looked annoyed.

"Yeah." I tried to pretend I didn't notice his agitation.

"We came all the way up here for two candidates? It would have been better to bring them to us instead."

"Oh, don't get so upset," his irritation was starting to affect me. "We wouldn't have known of Johns not making the guys tow the line if we wouldn't have come up here. Besides, I wanted to see Alaska."

"Alex," he sighed. "I suppose you're right. We'll start interviews later today then."

When breakfast was over we rounded up the men and ushered them back outside. After the morning drills, White called the men to attention. He told them I was here to assemble some teams for future jobs. If I asked anyone to meet with me they were to comply immediately. This brought brief and muffled comments but soon faded. Though they quieted the body language was thick.

He went on, explaining his disappointment with them and their lack of dedication and discipline. The morning drills would continue not only while we were here but every morning from here on out. If he found out they'd let their training slip again everyone would be sent packing. Dismissing the men, he walked me back to my office.

"I want to talk to you about your team before we call in Stevens." White started. "I've already told you I want a team under you like mine. Your team will consist of the best we've got but not all of our men have been to flight school or taken sniper training..." I nodded my understanding. "Your team will be trained in everything, not just their specialty."

"So, you want everyone to be interchangeable?"

"Exactly. Of course, we will send them out according to their strong suits, but if anything happens, someone else on the team should be able to fill in for anyone else."

"Well, I guess Stevens is out."

"No. Stevens is perfect. I suggest you put him under Intelligence Operative and EOD. We plan on training him for everything else. If you're ready, I'll fetch him."

White left to collect Stevens while I went over his file again. He didn't have any military training and his resume was pretty shallow. I knew we hired directly off the street at times, but I would have thought a person would need a better resume than what Stevens had submitted. Now I was going to ask him to be part of an elite team. White came in just as I was moving onto the next document, trailing Stevens behind him.

"Sit," I waved my hand at the chair.

"Ma'am," he greeted me before he sat.

"I have a few questions. First I don't see that you have any military background. I'd like to know how you came by your training since you don't list any of that in your resume."

"Yes, Ma'am," he cleared his throat and listed several other PMC's and soldier of fortune training camps.

"Why didn't you list these references?"

"I only took on those jobs to prepare me for this one and I didn't want White and Associates to think I couldn't hold a job."

That was explanation enough for me but I quizzed him on a few other things to make him sweat a little.

"Well, Stevens, I'd like to steal you from Team Brown and set you up as an Intelligence Operative for Team Grey," I finally told him.

"Ma'am?"

"You don't want to switch teams?"

"I don't know. I can't stand to be stuck in one place behind a desk. Intelligence Operatives normally sit at a computer, coordinating the mission from the outside."

"Yeah, I can understand that. I plan on using you for EOD as well, if that helps." I didn't want my first recruit to refuse so I changed to a more conversational tone. "I used to do data entry. Talk about boring." We laughed. Then I added, "I don't think there is anything about this job that's boring. All team members will be trained to do anything needed so you won't go into every job as the Intelligence Operative." I really did understand where he was coming from. I wouldn't want to be the one on the outside with every job. I wanted to kick some butt.

"I can deal with that," he said.

This satisfied White and he left us alone. As Stevens and I continued to talk, I found that I actually liked the guy. His posture became more relaxed and he started telling me more about himself. We talked mainly of his computer background and he was more than qualified to be on my team. He could easily be better at the computer thing than I was. I had hacked my way into many things but never took the risks he did. He told me stories of how he hacked into the local phone company, big corporations and other entities that would have had high security on their systems. I was impressed.

We concluded our meeting and decided that Stevens would come with me to the next compound and help me traverse the files. Hopefully this would speed things up.

When Stevens left my office I continued searching through the files to make sure I didn't have any other prospects. The only thing I accomplished was wasting time. There were no other candidates at this compound other than the "grunts." They weren't proficient in much more than the muscle part of their training. They did, however, show some promise and would be admitted on a trial basis. White helped me interview each man and left me at the end of the day to draw up the transfer slips. Everyone but Stevens would be starting a rigorous training program at a different compound.

After dinner, I searched out White and found him in his room. He said he'd meet me at the Iceberg for a drink.

There were a lot more men present than the night before. I counted over twenty men scattered around the building. I walked to the bar and ordered a coffee but when Joe brought it to me I went to a table to wait for White instead of sitting at the bar. Again, I found myself watching their lips and wasn't disappointed. My anatomy and my team were being discussed. The blonde cadet was present again and he started making his way toward me. Great, I thought to myself. I just can't win.

"Permission to speak, Commander Grey." He said. This caught me off guard but I granted permission.

"I want to apologize for my attitude last night. I know it's no excuse, but I'd had a couple beers too many."

"I'm glad to see you've remembered your manners, cadet. Apology accepted." Thankfully, White walked in and the cadet took his leave. I didn't know what else to say. In my crash course on how to behave, Red had told me to hold myself above the rest of the men, but I really didn't want to come off as a snob.

"What was that about?" White was apprehensive.

"An apology."

"Good." He ordered himself a coffee and returned to the table. His attitude wasn't businesslike but very informal. I might not have considered this unusual if we had been back at the office building, between jobs. However, we were doing interviews. Granted, we'd concluded them today but I still thought this was unusual.

I went along with it and learned a few things about White that I didn't know, but didn't give much of myself away. I wanted to talk with him like we normally would, but I couldn't bring myself out of job mode. Despite my unsociable position the conversation was not strained or stale. I was enjoying myself and so was White. Apparently he didn't mind that I didn't have much to say.

I returned to my room with a feeling of triumph. It felt like I'd just been on a first date. The thought of dating White made me jittery inside and I couldn't stop the little giggle that bubbled out of me. I was instantly angry with myself and forced the glee down. I couldn't explain why I would think this could be a date and any previous time we'd spent together didn't qualify. Maybe it stemmed from me being uncomfortable being too informal at this place. Date or not, I didn't want to get too worked up. If it had been a date he didn't go about it the right way. He should ask me to dinner and a movie or something comparable. I went to bed with more questions than answers.

I awoke with butterflies in my stomach. Sitting straight up I tried to remember my dream but realized it wasn't a dream that had me excited. We were done with the interviews and should be heading home soon. I rushed my shower and practically ran to White's room.

"I was just coming to your room for coffee," he said when he opened his door.

"So, when do we head home?" I didn't beat around the bush.

"You didn't make coffee this morning," he sighed as he led me into his room. He went to his coffee pot and I went to the small table and waited.

While the pot brewed he said, "I'm going to take over the drills today. These guys need to be whipped back into shape."

I nodded agreement. This was going to be interesting. Ever since he'd said he was as tough as Black and maybe more so I'd been watching for proof. I'd defended Black before and meant every word but didn't think White could be harder to please. White's attitude was tense so I drank my coffee in silence and repressed the question of home.

"Johns' replacement will be here today and we'll leave after I get him set up."

"You fired Johns?" This was news to me.

"Not yet. He'll have a choice of being demoted or getting fired when his replacement arrives. We can't allow our men to slack off like this and Johns is the responsible party here. He's obviously not disciplined enough to be in charge of a compound."

"All right, men," White said with authority. "Now that Commander Grey has made her picks the rest of you belong to me." His look was condemning as he continued on, becoming more strident until he seemed to be genuinely angry. White berated the men for a good ten minutes before he took a breath. Then he quietly told me I should sit out today but I declined.

We ended up more than half a mile away from the compound in front of an obstacle course. White and I watched as the men, including Johns made their way through it. It wasn't a pretty sight and by the time they were all done White was obviously fuming.

"This is a joke. If we needed any of these guys to do anything important, they'd all be too far out of shape to comply." He complained.

The men were still out of breath but White didn't allow a break. Immediately he led us all back at a faster pace than we'd come to the obstacle course. His uncompromising stance with these men helped me to understand what he'd meant when he said I wouldn't like training under him.

His training methods were different than Black's because Black expected you to do *your* best but White demanded that you do *his* best. I was step for step with White on the hard run back but the men were falling further behind with each stride.

It only took a few minutes to run back to the compound but the men straggled back in groups of no more than two or three. White's demeanor became more agitated with each small group that trailed in.

When all the men finally arrived White told them that they would be on a forced run after breakfast. The men all stood at attention and not one of them showed any signs of complaint.

"How long do you plan on running us?"

"You aren't invited this time."

"What? What if I want to run?"

"Then run, just not with us." His tone was matter of fact.

My nostrils flared before I could stop them so I added a glare for emphasis. He smiled his evil smile and I knew his enraged attitude was mostly for show. He still had his sense of humor, but was suppressing it to whip the men into shape.

White and the men were still gone when a plane arrived. Walking toward the lake to greet the new C.O. I saw Brown disembark from the plane too.

"Commander Brown," I greeted him.

"Commander Grey. I've heard this compound is in a shambles," he grinned. He introduced me to Johns' replacement and the three of us walked back to the officer's barracks.

When White finally returned I was already packed. He promptly instructed my team to pack and be at the plane in thirty minutes. As they scurried away, White went to brief the new C.O.

The flight home was tedious and seemed to take forever. I had always thought of the little guesthouse and my parents' house as home but now I caught myself missing my apartment at the offices of White and Associates and I was aching to get back.

When we finally set down on the roof of the office I practically jumped out of the chopper. I was excited to see my apartment. As we stepped into the elevator White told Brown to get Stevens and the other men situated and meet us in the office for a brief meeting. I was going to have to wait to see my apartment.

White and I sat in his office, talking about insignificant things until Brown arrived.

"So, where will we be flying off to next?" He slid past me and took a seat in front of White's desk.

"Do you want to chose?"

"Do I? You know it, girl." He was excited to tell me that we'd be going to Nevada next. It was where most of the people in his team were stationed. He explained to me that Nevada was a perfect place to do flight training and demolitions work. White seemed bothered that Brown had chosen that particular compound.

"Is that okay with you?" I wasn't in the mood to be defiant today.

"It's fine," his tone suggested otherwise.

"If you don't want..."

"I said it's fine," he cut me off.

"It's settled then. Get your bags packed, chicky. We leave in the morning." Brown stood and clapped his hands together.

I went to my apartment and was lounging on the couch when there was a knock at my door. I opened the door to reveal Colin and White standing in the hallway.

"Come in." I walked back to the couch.

Colin sat next to me while White stood behind us. "Here you go." Colin handed me an envelope.

Inside I found an identity packet. The woman's name was Emma Robertson, born and raised in the Midwest. The paperwork revealed her parents had died in a car accident a year ago and some minor details such as the name of her High School and some past job references. Then I saw the driver's license and it was me.

"What's this?"

"That could be you," Colin said in a game show host voice.

"So, you have another job for me?" I turned to look at White who just nodded in Colin's direction.

"Not yet. I just want you to be familiar with that identity, should the need arise."

"I'm going out of town for a couple of weeks," I told him.

"You didn't mention that," Colin said to White.

"She can be back here in a matter of hours, if need be."

"Well, I'm not even sure when we'll need you anyway." With that he stood and left White and I in my apartment.

"What job?" I asked White.

He shrugged his shoulders. "He just showed up at the office asking to meet with us. I have no idea what he's up to."

# Chapter Eight

The next morning I awoke in a great mood. I was actually excited to see the next compound. I wasn't feeling any anxiety like I had for the Alaskan trip. I think having Stevens to help with the paperwork made me more at ease. Having Brown with me instead of White didn't hurt either. No matter how hard I tried to control it, White always made me nervous.

I met everyone at the office half way through the morning and we all rode the elevator to the roof. Stevens and the other men I'd enlisted to be part of my teams were going to be transferred to the Nevada compound to begin their training.

Brown flew us away from the office but about fifteen minutes into the flight, he handed the controls over to me.

"You can use the practice," he said when I gave him a questioning look. I didn't argue. I liked flying the chopper. I didn't have much experience in either helicopter or planes, but I found I enjoyed the choppers more.

Brown took control once we neared the compound. He set us down, saying he was more comfortable if he did it. This was probably true, but he only did it to be ornery. Brown loved to pick on me or anyone else for that matter. He was perpetually happy and when he became sober faced you knew something was very serious. I had only witnessed it a couple of times in the past.

There was no welcoming committee when we stepped out of the vehicle so Brown drove us to our living quarters. The helipad was on the other side of the compound than the Officers Barracks so I tried to take in as much as I could on the way there. Our rooms were almost identical to the Alaskan compound, but I found a couple differences between the two buildings. This one was three stories instead of two and Headquarters and C.I.C. were housed on the first floor. Brown showed us which room he would be in and then we left Stevens at his room while Brown walked me to mine. He came in briefly to tell me that he'd be back later. He seemed really excited to be here so I didn't question anything. I managed to hang out in my room for almost forty-five minutes before I went to Stevens' room.

He allowed me in and offered me a seat at his small table. "I've never stayed in the Officers Barracks before." He had a big grin on his face.

"Just have to make the right friends," I chided him. "I hope I'm not bugging you, I'm just bored. Did you want to take a walk with me?" I hoped he would because I didn't want to wander around alone. This compound was much busier than the one in Alaska and I felt a bit out of place.

"Sure, I can show you around." He said.

"That's right. You were stationed here before you went to Alaska." I remembered from his file.

"Yeah, I started out here. I'm team Brown and had to undergo EOD training here to be accepted." Explosive Ordnance Disposal was training I hadn't undergone yet and didn't know if they'd get around to it.

"So, shall we?" I stood.

"It's a bigger compound than Alaska, do you think you could get us a vehicle? If not, we can walk."

"I can try."

We walked down to Headquarters together and I asked the cadets standing guard where we might find a vehicle to do some looking around. Immediately one of them was on the phone. Soon another cadet presented himself to us.

"Commander Grey." He said as he walked into the building. Then, he saluted me. I was caught off guard but returned the salute.

"At ease," I replied. "I just want to go look around before dinner."

"I'd be happy to drive you around, Ma'am," he sounded too eager, but I went along with it.

"Lets get going then." I had intended to follow him out the door but he and Stevens both waited for me to lead the way.

When we were all seated in the jeep I asked where Commander Brown had gone. The cadet driving us said that he didn't know and started with a tour guide tone, telling us all about the compound. Guard towers, sensors and cameras protected the fences. The compound contained a mock town for urban fighting training and explosives training. They had to rebuild the town about once a week because of the explosives. Eventually we made our way to the hangers. He started to talk about what they housed but continued to drive on by. I finally cut him and his tour guide tone off and told him to stop at the hangers. I thought I might find Brown there and I really wanted to let him know how I felt about being ditched.

"Yes, Ma'am." The cadet pulled up to the hangers, jumped out and ran to open my door.

"That's not necessary, cadet," I said as I got out.

"Only following orders, Ma'am," he replied.

"Whose orders?"

"Commander Brown, Ma'am." He looked ashamed to say it.

"He told you that you had to open doors for me?" I wanted to get to the bottom of this.

"Well..." he was obviously torn.

"Spit it out, cadet." I ordered.

"Yes, Ma'am," he seemed truly scared. "Commander Brown told us to treat you with the utmost respect because..." again he stammered.

"Because?" I asked.

"Because you are difficult otherwise." He didn't look me in the eye when he said this and gave special emphasis to the word difficult.

"Is that so?" I looked at Stevens who was grinning. "Do you think I'm *difficult?*" I asked him.

"I'm pleading the fifth," he teased. It hadn't taken long for Stevens to become comfortable with us. I suspected Brown had words with him as well.

I rolled my eyes and demanded that the cadet take me to find Brown. He moved as fast as he could and I began to find it funny. We quickly walked into the hanger and the cadet moved off to talk to some men standing near a jet. I didn't know we had a jet, I found myself thinking. Get back on track, I told myself. You're mad at Brown and you have to let him know. With the way the men were scurrying, I wondered what Brown had really told them. Soon Brown stepped around from behind the jet with a massive grin on his face.

"You found me," he raised his hands in surrender. They were covered in black grease.

I just shook my head and said, "What did you tell these poor guys? They are deathly afraid of me." I kept a stern look but was fighting to do it.

"I don't know what you're talking about," he played dumb, then successfully changed the subject. "You've met Sam?" I nodded my hello to Sam who'd been standing at attention this whole time. He'd shaved his beard and I may not have recognized him if it hadn't been for Brown. "And, Commander Grey, this is Lt. Will Malone."

I had been walking in Browns direction with Stevens trailing behind me until Will Malone made his appearance. My breath caught in my throat and I stopped dead in my tracks. Immediately I caught my mistake and made sure to keep my disapproving look trained on Brown. Then I looked back toward Will and said, "Nice to meet you." Only one other man had affected me like this and his last name was also Malone. I looked back to Brown and asked, "Any relation?" I already knew the answer but I thought I'd ask anyway.

"Not to me." He said with a sly look on his face.

"Not you, you dummy." I was flustered.

"Yep, brothers. Isn't that amazing?"

Will started to wipe his hands on his overalls then reached out to shake mine. I hesitated, but finally took his hand. "So, you know Rick?" he asked. I wanted to say, 'Duh, I'm a partner in HIS company.' But Will beat me to it, "I suppose you would," he gave me a smile that could make any woman melt but I held it together.

Brown cut in, "*Rick* and Will have been brothers for years." He said it as a joke, but I caught on. The people who knew White as White didn't always know that he was Rick Malone, brother to Will Malone.

"So, what do you do here?" I asked him.

"I'm a pilot but I don't actually work for White and Associates. I'm on loan from the government." I nodded but didn't know what else to say so the quiet quickly became uncomfortable.

"I suppose it's time for us to get cleaned up for dinner," Brown put in, catching the awkwardness. However, he was still grinning as if he'd done something crafty.

Brown commandeered the jeep the cadet had been chauffeuring us around in. He and I sat in the front and Stevens and Will sat in the back. There was no conversation all the way to the barracks. The four of us got out and Will walked across the street to his room while we walked into the Officers Barracks.

"What did you tell these guys?" I asked Brown when one of the cadets scrambled to open the door for us.

"Not much, just hinted at a few things." He smiled at me.

Brown was always doing something that he shouldn't be and I wondered what he was up to now. Yes, he'd told the men something about me that made them cringe when I walked by, but the Will angle was more interesting to me. The look he had when he introduced us told me he was up to something. Why else would he go out of his way to take me to this compound? He obviously knew Will Malone would be here. It was plain to see that he enjoyed presenting Will to me. Almost like a gift. Oh, shut up, I told myself. That's ridiculous. I'll just ask him, when we're alone. After we left Stevens at his door I asked Brown how long he'd be.

"Come on in, I'm just going to wash up," he held his room door open for me. When we both got inside he went to the bathroom and I sat at his table and waited for him to come back out.

"Are you going to yell at me some more?" He yelled from the bathroom.

"No," I didn't raise my voice as much as he had so he came out of the bathroom with a towel in his hands.

"I just want to know if Will Malone is the reason we came to this compound." I figured I'd come right to the point. Brown and I had become good friends and I was more than comfortable talking to him.

"Part of it. He's a friend of mine and I knew he'd be here. He's training some of my guys for me. Part of the reason I chose this compound was because it's kind of," he paused for a second, "mine."

"Yours?" I smiled.

"Yeah, most of my guys train here." He said.

"Then why didn't we come here when you were training me before?"

"It's too busy here. I needed to give you my full attention." He added a suggestive look for emphasis.

"Whatever," I rolled my eyes. "I think you have an ulterior motive here."

"All I'm going to say is, go with the flow." He got that sly look again.

Dinner came and went and I didn't see Will but I looked for him. I felt guilty but he most certainly was pleasing to the eyes. I reminded the feelings of guilt that I'd decided I was going to start dating. Then, they reminded me, I'd decided to start dating to prepare myself for White, and this was *his* little brother, after all. This could make things very awkward.

Brown caught me looking around more than once, so I quit and kept my eyes on my plate. It was pointless anyway because the mess hall was full of men. We finished dinner and Brown showed us where my office was.

After the brief tour, Stevens went off to do his thing and Brown and I went back to my room. Eventually Brown left me alone and I made my way to bed.

I awoke to loud voices outside. This was exactly what I'd expected at the Alaskan Compound. They must already be up and about for their morning drills and I had overslept. I hurried out of bed, started coffee and before I could get into the shower, Brown was at my door wearing a scowl.

"Did that awful racket wake you?" I feigned sympathy as I patted him on the back.

"Yes. This is another reason I trained you somewhere else." He pouted.

"It's good for you. Actually, you should be out there doing drills with them."

"Yeah... NO," he was emphatic. "What time do you want to start interviewing?"

"Probably as soon as they finish morning drills. You should get out there and get some exercise." I tried to take his coffee away from him but he wouldn't let me. Eventually I was able to kick him out so I could get ready.

I spent the next forty-five minutes alone with my thoughts, which circled around Will. I didn't even know him and yet I wanted to see him again. I kicked myself inwardly. Then another thought came to mind. White hadn't told me he had a brother. Did he have more than one, maybe a sister? I didn't even know if he had a mother. I guess I didn't know White that well after all.

Brown and I sat with Stevens during lunch and Brown was telling Grey stories. We'd heard planes all morning but it was quiet now and several men came walking into the mess hall. Their heads were held high and their attitude reminded me a lot of Red.

Will was in the front of the pack and looking good. My breath caught in my throat again and then our eyes met. He nodded his head in our direction and proceeded to get his lunch. I fought the urge to look away quickly and smiled at him, not knowing if his acknowledgment was directed at Brown or me or both of us.

"He's just training our guys but you could always add him to your team." Brown told me with raised eyebrows and a sly look.

"He's not a member of White and Associates. I can't add him. And, if I did, I'd have Stevens interview him."

"Great," Stevens cut in with an exasperated tone.

"What?" Brown asked him.

"Pilots are always so cocky." He said.

I caught the look on Browns face and quickly cut in, "Pilots aren't cocky, Stevens. They are just confident." I tried to make sure he caught my sidelong glance at the offended Brown. The look on Stevens' face after he realized his mistake was borderline horrified and it made me laugh.

"What's so funny?" I heard someone ask. I looked away from Stevens expecting to see White standing where the voice came from. It was Will and I had to fight myself not to let any emotion show. He set his food on the table and pulled up a chair directly across from me.

"Ms. Grey was just explaining to Stevens that us pilots are not cocky, we are just confident." Brown was enjoying this.

"We have to be. There's a lot riding on us. Not only are we in control of very expensive machinery, we usually have the lives of many men to be concerned with," Will explained to Stevens.

I'd heard it all before from Brown. I agreed with Stevens but I wouldn't admit it in front of a pilot. They were touchy about that kind of thing. I could easily understand the stigma placed on a pilot but I could equally understand them not wanting to be classed that way. I was quiet through the rest of our lunch. Will and Brown, on the other hand, were very chatty. I heard a couple of stories from their past and found my mind wandering to White. He and Will seemed to be very much alike, not only in appearance, but in attitude as well.

When we finished our lunches, Will said to me, "I'll see you in my class."

"No. I'm here to interview men for team assignments," I replied.

"Oh, that's a shame," he gave me a look I'd seen before and I knew he was trying to charm me.

"I'm sure we'll see more of each other." I was giddy because of the attention but he was too much like White to make me forget myself. Flirting with Will could be fun, but I didn't want him to get the wrong idea. I'd have to let him know, somehow, that my heart was not in it. However, if he and White were as much alike as they seemed, I was sure his heart wasn't fully engaged either.

Stevens and I spent the remainder of the day sifting through paperwork. When it was time we ate dinner with Brown and Will. I became more open as the dinner progressed and asked a few questions. I found out Will was the younger brother but was still a year older than I. He'd followed in his father's and brother's footsteps and joined the Navy and loved his job. He was cocky, but I think that was a result of his last name and not his job description. He definitely had charm and I found myself really enjoying his company. Rick Malone was the only sibling he had and yes, they did have a mother. He invited me for drinks after dinner and I politely declined. I then asked if every compound had a bar.

Brown was witness to all of Will's charms and my acceptance of them and explained away the bars as a place for the men to blow off steam. They were more than just places to get drunk, they were someplace the men could gather and be engaged in outside activities besides their job related duties.

"I don't think you should be going into the bar yet, anyway," Brown added.

"Why not?" This was strange. He was practically forcing Will and I together but now he didn't want me to go off with him. Was he trying to use reverse psychology?

"White told me about your run in at the bar in Alaska," he grinned at me.

I rolled my eyes and, of course, Will asked about it. I sat and listened to the exaggerated tale of me beating Sullivan to a pulp and more exaggeration about the run in with our guys at the Iceberg.

When Will looked at me a little funny I just shook my head.

"Yeah, I know Brown, too. How much of the story is true?" He smiled at Brown, knowing that he'd added to the story.

I went on to explain what really happened. Out of habit I went into debriefing mode and didn't leave out any details. I told him of Sullivan's reaction to me and I also told him of White's reaction to Sullivan. Then, of course, I talked about the mini play we were subjected to at the Iceberg, being sure to let him know that White and I didn't really take out the entire bar.

"So, why did you stop White from hitting Sullivan?" Will asked me. "I thought women liked it when men stood up for them." He had a strange look on his face.

"I can take care of myself. Besides, it wasn't necessary." I explained.

"So, I suppose you don't like it when men open doors for you." He said.

"On the contrary," Brown piped up. "She demands it."

"Only from you. You need the training." I teased him.

Will asked me one more time if I'd care to join him for a drink. Again, Brown objected.

"Well, in that case, I could go for one drink," I heard myself say. What was I doing? Then I heard myself ask Brown and Stevens, "Are you coming?"

They accepted the invitation and we all left the mess hall.

The four of us ordered our drinks and found a table in a corner. I knew Will didn't want the other men there, but I felt a need to be chaperoned.

The conversation was much the same as it was at dinner until Brown saw Sam playing pool. He said he was going to win some money, took Stevens with him and left me alone with Will. As soon as he was out of earshot the conversation changed.

"So, Brown tells me you're single. Is this true?"

"Well, yes. I'm not looking for anyone either."

"My kind of gal. I was hoping we could get to know each other better though."

"I'd like to get to know you, but I'll be frank," we were on our second drink and I felt the need to be honest all of a sudden. Normally this kind of honesty didn't rear its ugly head until after the fourth or fifth drink. "There will be no kissing." I was instantly embarrassed. "I can't believe I just said that. I better switch to coffee."

Will laughed. "At least you're honest. I'm disappointed but I think I can deal with that."

I became quiet in fear of saying something else stupid. I kept looking at Brown, hoping he'd come back but he didn't. Stevens had moved off to talk with some other men. The silence didn't last long before Will said, "You seem distracted."

"I'm sorry. I'm still a little embarrassed from what I said," I admitted. Funny enough, it helped me get past it.

"Do you want to play pool?"

"Oh, I've never been any good at the game. If you want to play I'll come watch. Are you any good?" I asked.

"Yeah," he grinned.

"Are you good enough to carry me against Brown and Sam?"

"Yeah. Do you want to go see if we can win some money?"

"Sure," I shrugged my shoulders.

When we reached Brown and Sam, Will asked if they'd like some fresh players.

"I know how she plays," Brown said. "But I know how you play too. We won't be playing for money tonight."

Will chided them while I ordered another round for us, making sure to get only soda for myself.

Brown still refused to play for money but we began a game anyway. He and Sam cleaned our clocks the first couple of games and I made sure to keep the drinks coming.

"You really suck tonight, Will." Brown was beginning to slur his words.

"Yeah, so play me for money," Will was also getting a little tipsy.

"Alright you two, that's enough. Are we going to play or not?" I cut in.

"Okay, okay." Sam took his shot and won another game for them. Standing behind me, Brown let out a holler and I felt a smack on my behind. Instantly I went into action and Brown was lying on the floor with a stunned look.

"I'm so sorry," I started to help him up. He was grinning from ear to ear.

As I pulled him up he put his hand on my shoulder and whispered in my ear, "I knew I'd get you with that. Thanks for the material. Now I don't have to make anything up."

I looked around and noticed the entire bar was watching us. Even Stevens had a stunned look. For the second time of the night I was horribly embarrassed.

Will had come to stand by my side.

"What's going on? Are you okay?"

"I hope you get a black eye," I said to Brown.

"Feels like I will," he was gingerly touching his cheek below his eye, still grinning. "I'm sorry, but the men were starting to question me. I had to make you do something to back me up."

"You're an asshole." I wanted to be angry with him, but I just couldn't when he was grinning the way he was. He took a good shot to the eye and wasn't complaining. "I really hope you get a black eye and it swells shut."

"Me too." We both laughed even though I fought against it.

"We better get out of here for the night," Will was looking around at the still quiet bar.

"I'm ready to go." I headed for the door with the rest of the men right behind me.

We parted outside and Brown walked back to the barracks with me. When we reached my room he invited himself in and asked me to make some coffee. I chided him and told him to make it himself but he begged, saying my coffee was the best. Flattery and guilt does get you places; I made him coffee.

"White didn't tell me he was going to pummel Sullivan." He had a strange look on his face.

"He said that we couldn't tolerate that kind of disrespect." I tried to explain it away. I didn't realize how much it was out of character for White until I'd seen Will and Brown's reaction. He was generally level headed and Sullivan's treatment of me had bothered him more than it should have.

"I see," was all he said. "So, you seem to have taken a liking to Will." His voice seemed to have a touch of regret in it.

"Yeah, I do. He's a nice guy. He reminds me a lot of White," I added to help his conscience.

"Well, they are brothers," he said. We continued to talk into the evening. Brown tried to get information out of me by asking sneaky questions about White. Where Will had been the main topic, now White was in there. I wished I had thought about how people would take it, before I had told them how White had acted out of character with Sullivan. However, I told myself, people would have found out anyway. There were witnesses, after all. I knew he had been standing up for me, but didn't put it together how much it really meant.

I hadn't even really talked to Colin about my infatuation with White so I wasn't sharing with Brown either. When he realized I wasn't going to admit an affair with White or admit to falling in love with Will he left me alone for the rest of the night. I had trouble falling asleep, but I did eventually nod off.

Stevens and I continued searching through the mountains of paperwork and had a nice pile of candidates in only a couple of days. Will, Brown, Stevens and I made a habit of visiting the bar after dinner, but I didn't allow myself any more alcohol. Brown's little trick seemed to bring up the level of respect the men gave me and it didn't hurt that he wore a nice shiner to remind them of that first night.

Early one morning I found myself on the phone with Colin. I really didn't know why I was calling him so I just asked him the same mundane questions.

He asked me if I'd memorized the identity he'd given me.

"Of course. I've been Emma Robertson in my off time."

"This is serious, Grey." He used my company name.

"Well, Commander, if you want to be that way about it. Yes, I've memorized her. Do you have a job for her?"

"I'm sorry, Alex," his voice lost its spirit. "I just think you don't give me enough credit," he complained.

"I must. I really do have the identity memorized. You're just too touchy."

"Well, I think I'm going to recall you for a job."

"Make sure it's worthwhile, I'm having fun here." I tried to lighten the mood. Colin sounded depressed and it was making me worry.

"I didn't think searching through paperwork was your thing."

"I don't know if I'd say that. It's tedious and boring, but I've been having fun with Brown and Will."

"Will Malone?" His voice became terse.

"Yeah. He's a great guy."

"Did you know he's Rick's brother," his foul mood returned.

"Yes, I do. I'm not that stupid. I don't know what's wrong with you but I've had about enough. First you think I'm underestimating you and now you're angry with me because I've made a new friend. What is going on?"

"I'm sorry. Now that the Admiral has given me more access to things, I worry about you more. And," he sighed, "I'm under a lot of pressure to fill your father's shoes."

"If he didn't think you were up to the job, he wouldn't have given it to you, you know that. As for me, when did you start worrying about me? I've found myself in some sticky situations before and you've never come to my rescue. What makes you think you have to do that now?"

"I've always watched out for you. You've just never put yourself into a position that's life threatening before you got this job so I've never said anything."

"Sorting through paperwork, memorizing a new identity and making friends with my partners brother is hardly life threatening. Sky diving lessons, scuba diving, rock climbing and a ton of things I did before I came to this company are more life threatening than anything I've done lately," I countered.

"Well, what I've got coming up for you could be extremely dangerous if you don't know your identity or if you step out of bounds at all."

"I see," now it was my turn to sound defeated.

"What do you mean, I see?" Colin was defensive.

"You aren't confident I can do the job, whatever it is."

"No," he was instantly apologetic. "It's not that at all. If you get hurt doing this job," he paused. "I'm the one putting you in this position."

"Not really," I felt better knowing he didn't think I'd go into this unprepared. "I'm the one who took this job and you had nothing to do with it. Besides, I'll be fine."

"I just want you to be careful." The call was ended shortly after this last comment and I began to look forward to my potential job.

Later that morning I started the interviews. Brown had recommended Sam and I had to tell him that he was already one of my picks. He was more than happy to join my team when I explained the additional training to him. When lunch rolled around I joined the men at the table. Will asked me if I'd like to go for a ride in the T-45 Goshawk. I was instantly excited and accepted without thinking first. I really wanted to go, but I didn't know if it was appropriate.

"Don't let her fly it," Brown cut in with a serious look.

"Why not?" My indecision was quelled with his statement.

"You aren't ready for that much plane yet and you know it." At first I thought he was kidding around like usual but realized he was sincere when I met his gaze.

"We'll be fine," Will reassured him.

"I'm serious, Will. Do not let her fly that thing."

Will looked as if he were going to argue in my defense so I quickly cut in and said, "It's okay. I don't need to fly it anyway. I would love to go for a ride though," I threw a cross look at Brown and stuck out my tongue for emphasis.

"Good. Meet me in the hanger at three and we'll take her up." He nodded a quick good-bye and headed for the door.

"Why don't you want me to fly it?" I asked Brown when Will was gone.

"I wasn't kidding when I said you weren't ready for that plane. It's for intermediate or advanced jet pilots. If you want to learn to fly that kind of plane you'll need to do a lot of training in a simulator first. If he's going to let you take the controls up there, don't. It's nothing like anything you've flown before." He was very serious.

I sighed and said, "I won't try to fly it, but when will you train me?"

He got a large grin and answered, "I won't. I'll have Will teach you."

I shook my head and left him standing there. I quickly walked back to my office. I had a couple of hours to kill so I finished my interviews but they didn't take long enough. I found myself walking circles so I forced myself to get on the computer and look up the Goshawk. I didn't want to look like an idiot if he asked me any questions up there. I became engrossed in the information I found and the time passed quickly. Soon it was time for me to start getting ready.

I had gotten into the habit of wearing my hair down lately but I pulled it back for my flight. I didn't want it in my face. After I did that I went down to Headquarters and asked the cadets if they could find me a ride to the hanger. They instantly jumped to help. I guess the bar scene didn't hurt anything but Brown's eye.

I was early getting to the hanger but I was so excited. This was a once in a lifetime chance for most people. Granted, I was in the position to make this opportunity not that unusual, but I wasn't going to throw it away.

As I got out of the jeep Will came up to me with an armload of equipment.

"Here," he handed it all to me. "Put this on and we can get going."

I did as I was told and found myself weighing about thirty pounds more. After I finished putting on the flight suit and headgear I walked over to Will who had been standing near the jet, watching me. He stuck his hand out to help me up the stairs to get into the jet.

"Sit in the back," he instructed. "If we were going on a training flight you'd sit in the front, but this is just for fun and the view is a little better from there."

Again, I did as I was told and before I knew it, Will was in the aircraft with me and we were taxiing down the runway. The pull of gravity as we lifted off the ground made my stomach do flips and I found myself smiling from ear to ear.

I watched as the ground grew smaller and Will asked if I could handle some fun. "Of course," I replied as our speed picked up.

Soon we were far enough from the ground that it no longer was the most interesting view. Will showed off by maneuvering the jet into seemingly precarious positions. I found myself holding my breath at times and laughing out loud at other times. Before I knew it, it was time to head back. When Will set her down on the runway I let out a sigh of regret.

"I know how you feel. I could stay up there forever." His voice held the same regret I felt.

"Thank you, Will. That is the most fun I think I've ever had." My adrenaline was still running high.

Will got out of the plane first and held his hand out once again to help me down. I was glad I took it because my legs were wobbly from the excitement and I almost fell over. He reached out with his other hand to catch me but I'd already regained my balance.

We took off our equipment, put it away, and jumped into a jeep. It was time for dinner and I was hungry. We laughed and talked about the flight all the way back to the mess hall and were still talking when we walked in. There was no line because we were late. Everyone was already at the tables, chatting and eating. We each grabbed a tray and I looked over to our table. I was going to give Brown an evil grin but instead I almost dropped my tray and I took in a sharp breath. My reaction made Will look toward the table and he said, "Ah, Commander White."

White was sitting at the table with Brown and Stevens. He had an undecipherable look. I hadn't expected to see him here and I immediately felt guilty for even talking to Will.

"I wondered how long it would take him," Will said as we got our food.

"What do you mean?" I asked.

"I called him and told him that you and I were getting along *very* well. I just wanted to see if he'd show up." Will gave me a knowing look.

"I'll bet you twenty bucks he's here because I have a job." I said, hoping Colin had already called him. Yet, at the same time, I wanted him to be here for me.

We found our way to the table and sat down. Will and White shook hands and both said it was good to see the other.

"What brings you here?" I asked White.

"You." He said, making my stomach turn.

"What?"

"I've come to collect you, Ms. Grey.  You have a job elsewhere." He said shaking his head in disdain.

I looked at Will and smiled, but inside I wondered what I'd done that was so wrong.  Will started to get his wallet out so I quietly told him to do it later.

White and I were nothing more than friends, but I did feel a bit like a cheater.  To have one person as the object of your infatuation for more than ten years helped to make it feel more permanent than it really was.  I couldn't help feeling disappointed I'd won the bet.

"When do we leave?" I asked.

"You've already talked to Colin so you should know he wants you to start ASAP."  Everyone at the table felt the tension, especially me.

"I'm not paying," Will whispered in my ear.  It gave me a chill and I grinned but when I looked at White I suppressed it.

"He just asked me if I'd be ready to do a job with the info he gave me earlier."  I didn't know if I should let on that I'd be using a separate identity.  "He didn't say he had a job for me *for sure*.  What is the job anyway?"

"So he didn't tell you what he wants you to do?"  White was shocked.

"No..." I didn't like his reaction.

"Well," he smirked.  "I'll tell you later."

"So, did you have a good time?" Brown cut in.  White's face became expressionless again and that was always a bad sign, but I didn't care.  He was being a jerk.  It wasn't like I'd gone off on a weekend getaway with another man and even if I had, he had no say.

"Yeah." I bragged up Will something fierce, telling them about all the twists and turns and how I didn't think I'd ever had that much fun in my life.  Then I added, for Brown, "I didn't even touch the controls."

The general mood lightened up after I picked on Brown.  White, however, ate quietly.  Stevens and Brown finished their meals first and left me alone with Will and White.  The tension returned somewhat and I decided to leave and let the brothers talk.  Both of them stood when I did.

"So, will we be leaving tonight or tomorrow morning?" I asked White.

"First thing in the morning."

Turning to Will, I said, "Thanks again, Will. I really did have a great time." I had an urge to hug him but he grabbed my hand and gave it a tender squeeze.

"It was my pleasure, Ms. Grey.    Anytime you want to do anything, you give me a call." Will was pouring on the charm, making me smile.

"You can count on it," I replied, noticing the sour look on White's face. As I turned to leave he added, "I'm sure we'll be seeing more of each other."

As an afterthought, I looked at White and added, "I'm going to go find the guys to say good-bye. I'm sure they are at the bar. Should I tell Stevens he'll be starting his training now that I'm done here?"

"You might as well. Don't stay out late."

Who did he think he was? Not even my parents had enforced bedtime for years. I raised my eyebrows at him and had my finger in the air before I decided against giving White a piece of my mind. I turned and left the mess hall, biting my bottom lip to keep it in place.

My mind reeled as I walked to the bar. I really liked Will, but seeing him and White together, I knew there was no comparison. I felt horrible for spending time with Will and yet at the same time was glad that I'd done it. The horrible feeling didn't last long when I thought of White's attitude toward me. Who did he think he was, trying to tell me how long I could stay out? I was a big girl and I was single in a compound full of men.

White and Will showed up at our table almost as soon as I'd sat down. I hadn't even been able to tell Stevens he'd be starting his training with the rest of the picks from this compound.

"I'll buy the first round." White offered and went directly to the bar. He came back with beers and shots all around. I had no intentions of drinking but I didn't want to do anything to hurt this sudden change of attitude.

We all drank down our shots to "Cheers!"

"So what's with the black eye?" White asked Brown.

"He grabbed my butt." I explained when the whole table of men eyeballed me.

"He did what?" His voice was tense.

"He told the guys here something about me that made them all afraid of me and grabbed me to get a reaction. I have to admit, it might not have been a bad idea."

"What?" He wasn't grasping it so I went on to explain Brown's intentions and White actually ended up laughing.

"Well, he knows you pretty well, but you can't react like that. You've got to think things through first."

"I know, but I will say in my defense, I *knew* it was Brown behind me and there was no other reaction. If you give him an inch, he thinks he can take a mile."

"Sounds like you know him pretty well, too." This topic lightened the mood further and Brown left to order us another round.

"None for me," I yelled after him but he brought another full round of shots. I knew I was going to find myself in trouble if I let them buy me any more. It wasn't long before Brown was asking who's turn it was to buy so I offered. Will objected and beat me to the bar. He returned with our third shot and after the toast I tried to take my leave. I knew the booze hadn't all kicked in yet and I wanted out of there before it did. They all protested that I hadn't bought my round yet so I made a trip to the bar. I gave the bartender a twenty to give me water in my shot glass and call it vodka.

"Since when do you drink something other than whiskey?" White asked.

"Since right now. Cheers!" I held up my shot glass and the men all followed suit. Stevens and Sam bought their rounds and thank goodness the bartender remembered my special order.

"Gentlemen," I stood. "I'm going to leave you to your drinking and get to bed." I wasn't slurring my words but I felt close to it.

"I'll be right there," Brown chimed in.

"Yeah, you wish." I chided him.

He stood up and came over to me and lifted me off the ground in a huge hug. I knew the liquor was certainly kicking in for him.

"I think I'll be right behind you anyway. I have to fly us out of here tomorrow," he said in my ear.

"Oh, I can get us home." I knew that would get a rise out of him.

"Yeah, you could." This surprised me so I told him he needed to go to bed right now. We laughed and he finally put me down on my own feet again.

"Good night all." I gave them a little wave and walked out the door.

# Chapter Nine

I hadn't been in my room more than two minutes when White came knocking on my door.

"What are you doing here?"

"Wow. Nice greeting." He smiled.

"You were the one with the attitude earlier," I was still peeved at him.

"Yeah, well, that's when I thought you'd taken the job Colin has in store for you." His smile turned evil.

"Okay, what is this job?"

"Dimitri has finally taken control of Gigi's and Colin wants you to start working there right away."

"What? The strip club?" I didn't entirely believe him. Colin wouldn't think I'd actually take a job as a stripper.

"Yep. That's what he said. Do you want to refuse to take the job?"

"What the hell do you think?" I didn't know if it was the alcohol or the thought of having to take my clothes off with everyone watching that was making me sick to my stomach.

"Are you sure? Colin said you've had dance lessons." I noticed the amusement in his voice but I played along.

"What else did Colin say?"

"That's about it," he shrugged.

"You tell Colin..." I had my finger pointed at him like I had started to do after dinner. "No, I'll do it myself." I went straight to my phone and started dialing Colin.

White came over and took the phone from me, laughing. "We thought if we could get you to strip it would be a miracle so Colin's lined up another job as a waitress instead."

"But still, in a strip club. I'll have guys all over me and that's why I quit the Skylight. I mean, look at Brown's eye. I don't do well with uninvited touches."

"I know, but you'll have to suck it up. It won't hurt you."

I cocked my head to the side, "Really? They won't be groping you. What about a bartender? At least I'd have the bar between me and *them*."

"No, he needs you to be able to go anywhere and a bartender is stuck behind the bar most of the night. We've got a couple of "regulars" in place so you won't be without backup."

I put my hand to my forehead. "I really don't want to do this."

"You can refuse. I just hope you don't. I can get extra out of Colin for a job like this, especially since he knew how you'd feel about it. You notice he left it up to me to tell you about it. Also, I doubt he's run this one past the Admiral." He was enjoying this way too much.

"Fine, but I expect hazard pay for this one and I mean a *big* bonus."

---

White retrieved me early the next morning and I could tell he wasn't feeling too well. Brown was in about the same shape so I kept my mouth shut for the flight back to the office.

We rode the elevator down to my apartment and White stepped out with me. I gave him a questioning look and he said we needed to go over the job a little more while I packed.

"Pack? For what?" I was just going to go apply for a job today.

"Yes, pack. You've taken on a separate identity and you have to act the part. You do know your identity, don't you?"

"Yeah. I'm Emma Robertson. I'm from the Midwest and my parents are dead," I rattled off.

"It's more than that. You don't just have to know who you are playing, you have to become her. She has a personality that doesn't belong to you but you have to make it yours."

"Okay, what kind of personality does she have?" I rolled my eyes.

"This is serious. Colin is putting you deep into the workings of the Russian Mafia. They'll check you out, especially if you don't seem to fit. You are not a Midwest girl and it shows."

I didn't say anything. I knew he was right and I had given it some thought. I just felt silly trying to be someone else.

"Colin didn't give you much of a back story, other than your parents so you'll have to create it yourself. You might not need it, but it'll help you become Emma."

"I have actually given it some thought. I'm thinking she'd be a little naïve, coming from a rural area to a city." I was more inexperienced than I like to admit so this may not be that much of a stretch.

"Good start. Colin wanted to meet before we set you up in your new apartment and he should be here soon."

I left White in my living room and went to pack some clothes. He reminded me to be sure to pack what I thought Emma would wear.

"Oh, and pack enough to make it look like it would be everything you own," he added.

Colin arrived before I was finished and White let him in. I heard an unfamiliar voice so I stuck my head out of my bedroom.

"Emma, this is Michael Evans. He'll get you set up in your new apartment." Colin introduced me to the man standing next to him.

Mr. Evans was an older gentleman with graying hair at the temples. He wore a crisp suit and an equally crisp expression.

"Mr. Evans." I walked over and shook his hand.

"Emma," he pulled me into a hug and rubbed his hand down my back. This caught me off guard but I didn't budge and gave him an equally affectionate hug.

"I've found you an apartment. Are you ready?"

"Almost. I shouldn't be too long." My tone was affable though he made me nervous. I wondered how closely I was going to have to work with Mr. Evans. His touchy demeanor was off putting.

I finished packing and lugged two large bags from my room. Mr. Evans took a bag from me and Colin put a cell phone into my free hand.

"Contact us only through Evans, unless it's an emergency and you need to be pulled out. I need you to keep your eyes and ears open for anything that will help us get Dimitri and Grigori."

"We'll lock up," White added as I followed Evans out the door. I hope they don't snoop through my apartment, I thought.

Evans put my luggage into the trunk of his car but his habit of putting his hand in the small of my back bothered me. I wasn't looking forward to being cut off from everyone and he didn't make me feel any better with his touchy feely ways.

Once inside the car Evans said, "My number is programmed into your phone." We pulled out of the parking garage and all was silent until we reached my new apartment.

Evans had driven me to one of the worst parts of town. The building had to be the most neglected on the block and I was appalled. At least my apartment was on the bottom floor of the rundown building. I tried to make myself feel better.

"We've set up an interview for this afternoon. Let's get you unpacked and then you can catch the bus to Gigi's. Don't worry. You'll be fine. My friends will look out for you. I know it's hard being away from your hometown but you'll be glad you moved here." He was giving me hints of Emma's expected personality and it sounded as if I was to play a scared little girl.

Mr. Evans helped me unpack and this made me uncomfortable as well. He found my most conservative outfit and instructed me to put it on for my interview. I did as I was told as he finished unpacking my belongings. When I came out of the bathroom he ushered me out the door so I wouldn't be late for my interview. He was starting to make me feel inadequate and scared. Instead of taking my normal defensive stance I went with the flow.

Gigi's was downtown, quite some distance from my new apartment, so the bus ride wasn't a short one.

I had to walk only a block from the bus stop to get to Gigi's front door. I walked with purpose until I was within a few feet of the establishment and my confidence dropped. Tentatively, I opened the door and stepped in. I really didn't want to see naked women running around and figured Emma would feel the same. I kept my head down as I walked in but when I looked up I was full of angst and my hands started to sweat. I'd never been in this type of establishment before and it was harder than I'd expected.

I made my way to the bar and said I had an interview for a waitress job.

The woman behind the bar eyeballed me up and down and with a scowl she pointed me toward the back of the building. "Go to the office."

Maneuvering through the tables and past the stage I entered a tight hallway. The walls and carpeting in the hall didn't change from the rest of the building. The wallpaper was a velvety deep red with carpet to match. The deep red color of everything kept the light subdued and unnatural. Labeled doors broke up the walls on either side of the hall. There were dressing rooms, restrooms and one unlabeled door. I knocked on this one, hoping it was the office.

It swung open slowly to reveal a large man. His body filled the entire frame and he stood there just looking at me.

"Uh," I stammered. "I have an interview for a waitress job?" It wasn't hard to fall into the personality of Emma Robertson.

"Let her in," I heard a voice come from behind the huge man. He stepped aside to allow me access and I walked in with my eyes on my feet.

"Miss?" The man asked in a strong Russian accent. I looked up and immediately recognized him as Dimitri. My stomach ached.

"Robertson." I replied timidly.

Dimitri was clearly sizing me up.

"You would like to waitress?"

"Yes sir."

"You can't dance?"

"No, sir."

"You will learn." I screamed inside. I would not take my clothes off in public. Panic set in.

"I… uh…" my stammering was unconscious. "I'd rather wait tables, if I could." I felt tears of dread well up into my eyes.

"I like my girls on stage to be more confident, but you will learn." Dimitri ordered. "Here," he walked to a closet in the back of the room and pulled out an outfit. "Put this on and I'll see if you'll do for a waitress until you learn to dance."

I took the clothes from him and hurried out the door to the bathroom. I was thankful he didn't make me change in front of them. After I'd gotten dressed I checked myself out in the mirror. I was slightly uncomfortable with the amount of skin it showed but it covered the three most important places so I walked from the bathroom back toward Dimitri's door. I knocked, unsure if I should just walk in. The large man opened the door and I stepped through. I was made to do a slow circle in the middle of the room and finally passed inspection.

"You'll do. You can start right away. Talk to Katryna behind the bar and she'll get you set up."

Other girls were starting to filter in as I walked toward the bar. One passed me in the hallway on her way to a dressing room where some quiet voices were leaking through the door.

"Mr. Prutko told me to find Katryna," I said in a small voice when I reached the bar.

"He did hire you." She also had a Russian accent and she didn't try to hide any of her distaste.

Several hours into my shift I was back into the swing of things. I took note of every face in the bar but no one was familiar to me. If Colin and White had men here to watch over me I didn't know who they were.

Dimitri stayed in his office for the rest of the evening so the only thing I accomplished was getting acquainted with the other waitresses.

At closing time I was collected, along with the other girls, to meet with Mr. Prutko. He held out his hand and the girls started handing him their tips one at a time. I looked over and some of them wore disgusted looks.

"We never had to do this before and I won't do it now. I quit," one of the girls objected and started for the door. The two big goons inside the room with us blocked her way until Dimitri told them to let her go. He then added that he wanted his uniform back. She stormed out, followed by one of the goons but the rest of the girls were straightening their bills and handing them over. Dimitri counted the money placed on his desk then gave some back to the waitress or dancer who'd placed it there then he moved onto the next girl. When it came my turn I handed him my tips and watched him count it. He then explained to me, because I was new, that half of my tips went to the rental of my uniform for the night. What a crock, I thought to myself but kept my mouth shut. I even managed a "Thank you," when he gave me back some of my tips.

"Now, that's the kind of respect I like to see. Pay attention, girls. And not even from a proper Russian upbringing," he mused to himself.

Evans called my cell phone as I rode the bus back to my horrid apartment. He wanted to see how my first night went and I told him about the tips.

"Mr. Prutko has to pay for the uniforms somehow," he defended him. He then went on to tell me to go straight to my apartment and he'd be by in the morning.

Evans showed up the next morning as promised and gave me a bug to plant near or in Dimitri's office. Then he took me grocery shopping and warned me to stay inside my apartment after he left me.

Easy enough for him. I'm sure he had a computer and a T.V. where ever he was going. My two-room apartment consisted of one larger room and a bathroom. The bathroom was barely clean and the primary room only had the general kitchen appliances, a bed and a table. Not even a book in the place and I'd not thought to bring any with me.

I hopped on the bus for my second night at work. Dimitri remained in his office and I wondered if he ever came out. How was I supposed to plant a bug with him in there all the time? At the end of the evening when we were all brought into the office to share our wealth I purposely dropped some of my quarters on the floor. Thankfully, one of them rolled to the bookshelf near the wall and I was able to place the bug underneath.

I spent the rest of the week going through the same routine. I was able to recognize the regulars and had my suspicions on who was sent to watch over me. Dimitri rarely came out of his office but it didn't really matter because I had the bug in place.

Most of the men were polite enough to their waitress because they had plenty of opportunities with the dancers, but there was an exception. He told me his name was Sal. He took an instant liking to me and refused to keep his hands to himself.

More than once I faked an unaffected smile after his hands made contact with an inappropriate part of my body. Eventually, I took a breather in the bathroom for a few minutes. I'd never been able to stand being fondled and it was taking everything I had not to break his arm. I only hoped Dimitri would make plans for the bug to hear. I wanted out before they tried to make me dance.

Evans didn't make contact for several days and my calls went unanswered. What if I had an emergency I thought to myself. I was about to break a rule and give White a call when Evans finally called me back.

"Is everything okay?"

"Yes, I was just wondering what was going on," I explained my previous calls.

"No changes. My men are still in place so don't worry if you can't reach me. If you need them, they are always close by."

"How much longer do I have to be here?"

"I can't answer that." He then told me he had to go and hung up. Having no contact with White or Colin was really beginning to concern me and I was still considering contacting them.

After pacing my apartment for several minutes, I decided against it for today but that didn't mean I wouldn't call tomorrow.

I forced myself to go back to Gigi's and Sal made his appearance early in the evening. He'd become a regular at my tables.

He stopped at the bar and I hoped he'd stay there, but all he did was order a round for the bar, making sure to tip Katryna heavily. He took a seat at one of my tables. He kept me from my other customers and I had to literally pry his hand from my arm so I could continue to work. Shortly after this I was called into the back office.

Katryna had gone back to complain about me. Dimitri demanded I explain to him why my customers were being neglected so I told him of Sal's attentions. I kept my eyes on the ground as I spoke and he ordered me to look at him when I addressed him but when I did my cheek was met with a hard slap from one of his goons, knocking me to the floor. I was on my feet almost as soon as I hit the ground but remembered myself before I lashed out.

I felt blood trickling down my face but didn't dare wipe it away.

"I'm sorry Mr. Prutko," my voice wavered but I managed to make my anger sound like fear.

"Neither of you are to lay another hand on her." He admonished his men. "Well, it's a good lesson all the same," he directed toward me. "I will speak with Katryna. Mr. Novikov is a valued customer and you'd do well to tend to all of his wants. Now go clean yourself up."

I made my way to the bathroom, shaking from the pent up energy I had to suppress. I had a nice cut on my cheek and it was going to bruise but probably not scar. I washed away the blood and headed back to work.

Katryna wore an evil smile when I returned. I couldn't help it, I smiled right back at her. This seemed to throw her off guard and I was hoping to see her in a dark alley sometime soon.

One of the regulars stood from his seat when he saw me but another man stopped him dead in his tracks. Now I knew who'd been watching out for me. Sal also noticed the wound on my face and asked what happened. I told him I fell because I couldn't think of an appropriate lie, but he took it with a smile and reached up and touched my cheek gently.

"It would be a shame to damage a face like yours," I blushed and was instantly mad at myself. I was beginning to act too much like Emma Robertson should and I was keenly afraid of losing myself in all this mess.

Sal made a habit of touching my cheek with a smile that made me uneasy. It got to the point where I was unable to wait on any other customers. However, I was never called into the back room again and Sal was very generous with his tips that I wasn't allowed to keep.

Katryna became increasingly hostile toward me until she cornered me outside as I walked to the bus stop.

"Who do you think you are?" she accosted me.

I was in Emma mode and played the part. "I don't know what you mean."

"Mr. Novikov is *my* customer and I don't appreciate you stepping in where you don't belong."

"I'm sorry. He just sits at my tables, I can't help it."

"Well, I can. If you're ugly, he'll lose interest." She threw a punch that connected with its mark. I continued to play the scared girl part with a bloody nose and fell to the ground, covering my face. Katryna started to kick me as I lay there. She kept kicking and kicking and there was no one coming to save me. When I realized this I jumped up and nailed her a good one right across her jaw. She went down and didn't move for a few seconds but eventually staggered to her feet. I wasn't finished with her so I gave her time to get oriented.

She stood with a renewed energy and came after me in a head-long charge. I stepped aside and could have grabbed her and finished the fight right there, but my wits returned and I knew Emma wouldn't know most of the moves I did so I grabbed her by the hair and flipped her back to the ground. I considered kicking her while she was down but always thought that was the cheap way out so I let her get up again.

This last fall had only knocked the wind out of her and I wanted revenge for the time she'd told on me and all the other times she'd tried to get me into trouble. She screamed in frustration as she came at me again. This time I didn't move and let her come in and knock me to the ground. She was a little bigger than me but after a couple of punches to my side I was able to flip her over and I sat on her chest with my knees on her elbows. She thrashed under me but was unable to get away. I proceeded to slap her instead of punch her. I wanted to beat her bloody, but thought I'd cause the pain without leaving the marks so she couldn't tell other people I knew how to fight. I did throw in a couple of punches to her kidneys, just for good measure before I felt myself being lifted off of her.

"What's going on here, girls?" I heard a man's voice from behind me as I struggled half-heartedly. I watched another man come around to help Katryna up. They were the two men who'd been sent to keep an eye on me.

"Nothing," she spat at them and yanked her arm away. I held my tongue but directed a vicious smile at Katryna. I couldn't help myself, I'd enjoyed beating on her. She was lucky I wasn't able to show her what I was really made of. Visibly taken aback by my ferocity she turned to walk away. I watched with triumph as she hobbled away, first gingerly touching her face then holding her side.

The man who'd been holding me put me down and I walked away without a word. The next few nights at work, Katryna was a bit slower than normal and I got a little satisfaction from it. Apparently she didn't tell a soul about our run in and I was thankful for that.

A few days later, Evans made his morning visit but told me to pack things up. I did as I was told and didn't ask questions. After he pulled into the parking garage of White and Associates he unloaded my luggage from the trunk and then sped off.

I made my way to the seventh floor office. I was so happy to be back in my world and out of Emma Robertson's miserable life. I chatted briefly with Gabriella before I went in to see what White needed.

"Colin called this morning." White didn't make any effort to hide his frustration.

"And?" I asked.

"Apparently you got into a fight with one of Dimitri's girls?"

"She attacked me so I defended myself," I knew I hadn't been wrong. "I even let her beat on me a little so I wouldn't give myself away. Plus, I didn't leave any marks on her and there were no witnesses except Colin's men."

"I'm sorry, Alex. I'm not upset with you. Colin said all he really needed was for you to plant the bug but kept you there in case something else came up."

"What!" My voice went up several octaves.

"Yep. So to make it up to you he's included a substantial bonus."

"I can't believe this! That bug has been in place since my second day of work. Is the bonus above and beyond what I could expect for having to work in a strip joint or did he just keep me there to justify *that* bonus?"

He handed me an envelope. "White and Associates is satisfied and if you want more you will have to approach Colin on your own."

I opened the envelope and pulled out my check. It was much more than I'd expected.

"As long as we're getting paid," I sighed. I wanted to remain angry but the amount of the check had caught me off guard. I slid it back into the envelope. I certainly wasn't going to complain now that I'd seen the zero's.

"We can finally get on with our training op now. I've been putting it off for months so we could include you." His aggravation had faded as he moved from his desk to a filing cabinet.

I wondered what kind of training I was up for next. Maybe I'd be learning how to blow things up.

White returned to his desk with a file and plopped it down. He reclaimed his seat and began flipping through the pages. After he found what he was looking for he passed it across the desk to me.

It was the plans for the Big Horn compound. I recognized it by the distinctive diamond shaped layout. This compound was used to train for mountain warfare, high altitude training and other related things.

"What will I be doing here?"

"We are going to do an infiltration." He explained this type of training operation was done quite frequently. However, they'd been putting them off since I'd joined the team.

"We will discuss the operation later today in the war room. Everyone else knows their part so I wanted a private meeting with you to explain our expectations. Since this is your first mission with the whole team you should know everyone is expected to be involved in the planning." I assumed he meant Team White.

"You and Blue will be our eyes on this mission." He slid the rest of the folder toward me. "Decide where you'd like to set up. Also, we will be using two or three of your teams to help out with this one."

"I didn't get everyone interviewed," I fretted.

"But, you did get your list done. I've taken the liberty of assembling the teams while you were away."

"Oh," I was a little disappointed. It was the paperwork I wasn't all that thrilled with. Going to the compounds and interviewing the men wasn't all that bad.

"I know you might have liked to do this on your own, but I needed your teams right away. They need to get their training in so they can start jobs," he apologized.

"That's okay," I shrugged. "I will get to meet my men though, won't I?"

"Of course. Eventually." White talked more of the operation as I skimmed through the folder.

"You've not given me much time to go over this," I complained.

"I know, but you've got to learn how to come up with a plan quickly anyway."

"I better get started." I rose from my chair.

"Here," he tossed his keys at me. I almost dropped the file as I reached out to catch them. "Use C.I.C. The rest of us will be there in a few hours."

# Chapter Ten

When I walked into White's apartment I was reminded of how clean and organized it always was. I kept up on my apartment but I was a woman. Black's place was more like a bachelor's. It wasn't dirty but it was cluttered with various items. The neatness of White's quarters made me want to snoop. There was nothing laying out that gave me much insight into the private life of Rick Malone.

Standing just inside the door, I took it all in instead of succumbing to the urge to dig through everything. I forced my legs to take me directly to C.I.C.

Once inside, the computers called my name. It had been such a long time since I'd seen technology I almost forgot why I was really here. White's apartment was full of distractions and temptations but I managed to focus and got right to work.

I pulled up the real time view of the compound and instantly knew where Blue and I should set up. The compound was situated in a small valley and the hills made great cover for a sniper/lookout. I found opposing perches that allowed a full view of the compound if we worked together. I agonized over my decision for a short while before I agreed with myself that the two spots were the best places for us.

I took the remainder of my time to figure out every aspect of our attack. I was still wrestling with some of my decisions when White walked in.

"So, how's it coming?"

"Well, if I'd have had more time I'd be more sure of the plan but here it is so far." I handed him the printout of the compound I'd been writing on.

"You planned the whole thing?" He was surprised.

"I thought that's what you wanted." He'd taken a seat at a desk and was looking over my plan. I walked to him so I could explain it a little better. "Blue and I will be on opposite hills so we can take in the entire compound and inform the teams of any movement or changes," I pointed to our perches from over his shoulder.

"Those would seem to be the best places," his voice was amused.

"What," my voice held no amusement. I'd been working hard for the past couple hours and didn't appreciate him taking that for granted.

"Nothing," he caught my lack of humor and changed his tone. "I didn't expect you to plan the entire offensive. However, this has merit," as he said this Brown and Red walked into the war room. White swiveled in his chair and called Red over.

"I think all we need to do today are some minor adjustments," he stood and invited Red to take his place.

"I thought you said you were too busy to plan this one alone," Red commented with raised eyebrows.

"I didn't do it," White inclined his head toward me.

"Explain it to me," Red's eyes were curious as he took the chair White had given up.

Blue, Black and Green arrived just as I finished explaining my scribbles to Red.

"It certainly has potential and a little polish seems to be all it needs," Red gave me an approving look as he handed me my paperwork. "You've got promise in the planning department," he told me. This was the biggest and best compliment I'd ever received from Red and I was shocked. Maybe he'd start to warm up to me a little. I admit, I wasn't overly friendly to Red either, but until he made the first move toward friendship, I wouldn't budge. This, however, could be that first move.

White called the meeting to order by telling the men to find seats, "Ms. Grey will lay out the plan and we can make suggestions when she's finished."

I didn't let my nervousness show as I explained how I thought this mission should proceed. I met with surprisingly little resistance to every thing I suggested. Blue came up to me after some small changes were finalized.

"I've got our equipment in the chopper. We should be going."

"Already?" I didn't expect to be leaving immediately. I hadn't even been to my apartment since returning from my job at Gigi's. I'd been gone a long time and wanted to spend some time at home.

"Yeah. We'll get set up and start scouting the area before the other teams arrive. We'll give a detailed report before they move in. Then any last minute changes can be made if needed."

I followed him and Brown to the roof and after several refueling stops I finally found myself repelling from the chopper a safe distance from my designated roost. Despite the dark, I made good time and caught sight of lights from the compound in less than thirty minutes.

Settling in and getting as comfortable as possible I started making mental notes. I'd studied all the compounds and knew this one had two gates, but I only had a clear sight of one. The compound's Headquarters blocked my view of the second gate. Otherwise, I had an excellent view of the compound. There were two guards posted at this gate and I knew I'd have to keep track of when they changed out. I noticed six other posts around the compound and several roving guards. I made note of all movement patterns, isolated and congested areas and other things such as lighting placement. At least I wouldn't have to wait till dark to get the full effect of lighting. In no time I knew every nook where a number of men could stand and be under the cover of darkness.

When a few hours had passed and I hadn't heard anything from Blue I changed my focus of interest. I scanned the area where he should be for several minutes before I found him with my night vision. The tiniest little movement caught my eye and I reasoned it was Blue.

He was well disguised. I only became sure of my discovery when a voice crackled in my ear.

"Watch the compound." Though it startled me I didn't make any sudden movements. Slowly I returned my attentions to my proper target.

It was still dark when the gate guards finally switched out for fresh eyes. I reasoned they were on four-hour shifts but would wait until the next change out to consider that as fact. I could tell the new faces were relaxed in their routine by watching the way they habitually performed their duties. They wouldn't be looking for any outside interference. Again, the voice in my ear startled me when it demanded a report.

I quickly rattled off my observations and was rewarded with Blue's report of the other side of the compound. It was obvious we had overlapping views, which was what I'd hoped for.

When he completed his report I was tempted to ask him how long we'd wait until the other teams arrived but I assumed the less radio contact the better.

Every four hours I heard the familiar voice in my ear, demanding a report. This went on for three days. Monotony set in and I'd resigned myself to only hearing Blue's voice in my ear from now until the end of time when White's familiar voice touched my consciousness. I felt giddy.

His voice always gave me a warm apprehensive feeling but it was intensified being so close in my ear. The mind-numbing surveillance had come to an end and that fact probably helped heighten my senses a little.

"Report, Blue."

Blue included my reports as well and when he finished White asked, "Anything to add, Grey?"

"No, sir," was my only response.

"We are in position and will move in at twenty-two hundred hours. Resume your watch."

"Yes, sir," Blue and I answered in unison.

The reports back and forth continued until I caught sight of a troop of men moving in from the west. I knew the plan was to take out all the stationary guard posts first so I scouted until I saw the other groups of men surrounding the compound. They'd have to all strike at once to make this work. If any of the compound guards got off a distress signal it would have to be called off. We wouldn't use deadly force but the troops we were attacking would.

Team Grey was split into six teams of five men to be led by each of the available partners. Their first task was to take out the stationary perimeter guards. There were six posts with two men defending them. As soon as those positions were in our control the teams would converge and take out the gate guards. It was mine and Blue's duty to make sure the men could see around all corners at all times. Then they would systematically take control of each building until the compound was under our command.

The six teams moved together and had the perimeter in their control within seconds. It was a beautiful sight to watch them move. They almost reminded me of a flock of birds or a school of fish. Yet, a flock or school moved in a flowing motion and my teams all moved simultaneously.

With the perimeter and gates under control, the six teams converged again. The men now had sixteen captives they had to control. I watched as they were bound and gagged and left near the outer fence with one team of our men to guard them.

My eyes darted over the entire compound as the teams split again. Each had a designated building they would take over.

Green and White's teams made their way to Headquarters while the rest of the teams went to take positions near their assigned buildings. I continued to scour the darkness and caught sight of two men exiting the bar. They were moving directly toward Red's team who were on their way to take command of the bar.

"Red, two men straight ahead," I warned. I watched Red's team stop dead in their tracks and slowly shift into deeper shadows. As the two men approached I worried one or both of them would spot my men standing just out of reach but they didn't. I couldn't tear my eyes away from the scene. The two men developed more substantial shadows that slowly closed the distance. Within seconds they were under our control and being shuffled toward the rest of our captives.

I went back to my surveillance of the entire compound and caught movement near Headquarters in my night vision. White and Green's teams were standing by in ready positions so I assumed what I'd seen was a member of their team. I counted heads and discovered they were one short. I looked again for a glimpse of some more activity but there was none until the compound went completely dark. There was a flurry of activity by our men. They all moved in and took their buildings in a synchronized manner. I caught sight of that same movement and watched more carefully. It was Green. He'd been standing near the building all the while. Somehow he'd blended in even though I had the benefit of night vision and knowing the plan. He'd been standing by an electrical box and I knew he'd cut all the appropriate wires to shut down the compound.

After the power and communications were shut down the take over was almost instantaneous. I felt badly for the men stationed here because this made them all look bad. However, I knew it needed to be done to keep them on their toes. Plus, I reminded myself, the attacking teams were composed of the best we had.

I watched them herd the POW's toward the mess hall in small groups. I'm glad I'm not one of them, I thought, with my hands tied up and duct tape over my mouth. Then I heard White's voice, instructing Blue and I to join them at the compound. This halted any further thoughts of the mission. I'd always been fond of his voice but because of the earpiece I could almost feel his breath on my neck. These thoughts led to other thoughts and pushed out all other topics while I made the trek down the hill.

I didn't pull myself from my daydreaming until I was at the entrance to the mess hall. I took a deep breath and pulled on the door so it was just wide enough for me to pass through. Quietly I made my way to White's side. A few men noticed my approach but White didn't see me until I was next to him.

"Did you run," he asked me.

"No," I thought he was referring to my prompt appearance.

"You're flushed. Are you okay?" He looked at me deliberately.

His concern was enchanting and I fought to keep my sigh inaudible. The deep breath didn't help to calm me and I was unable to speak. Even if I had the ability, I wouldn't know what to say. I quickly shrugged my shoulders and turned away hoping he wouldn't ask any more questions. I turned my attention to the men grouped along the north wall. This helped me reclaim my sanity.

"That didn't take long," I motioned to the men still with their hands tied and mouths taped. I turned back to White to get his reaction. He didn't look satisfied but followed my change of subject.

"As soon as Blue joins us we'll let these guys know what's going on." Just then the lights came back on and soft humming of electrical appliances resumed.

"Good. Green should be back any minute now." He said this to himself as he looked around the room.

The mess hall was full of men who were either standing at ease, milling around or tied up. I felt out of place so I found a corner and stood quietly until Blue and Green each made their appearance. I would have stood in my corner watching the scene if I hadn't noticed White looking around for me.

My partners were fully assembled and stood at attention as White introduced me to my team. I was surprised he chose to introduce me before finishing up the mission.

However, it was quite impressive to see thirty men, standing at attention suddenly salute me. The pride was almost overwhelming.

"Nice to finally meet all of you," I began. Sam had led the one team not led by a partner but only his and Stevens faces were familiar. Every other face was new to me. "I appreciate the great job you did here." I looked at White to signal I had nothing more to say.

Everyone returned their attention to the captives as if an afterthought. With a flourish of his arms indicating their situation White explained to them this was why they couldn't become too comfortable with their positions. He went on for some time before he allowed them to be released and return to their duties. Team Grey was told to help restore the base to normal and the C.O. was held back for a meeting with Team White.

I expected White to chew him out and possibly fire him but the meeting was very civilized and didn't include any ramifications. The C.O. was shamefaced and apologetic as White reminded him of the lecture he'd given the entire group just minutes before.

"You seemed to be pretty easy on him," I commented after everyone had disbursed.

"He's been keeping up on their training and we haven't done a test like this for over a year. It's my fault the men have become lax. Now that we've shaken up the Alaskan compound and this one, word will get around and none of the compounds will be easy targets for several months." He took a deep breath and looked at me like he just remembered something.

"What?" His gaze made me self-conscious.

"You aren't flushed anymore. Are you sure you feel okay? You've been working for more than a month without a break."

I gave a nervous laugh and assured him I was just fine. I knew White worried about me from time to time but he'd never shown it so openly before for such a small matter. I was reminded of the glance he'd stolen in the car while I was bent over searching for plane tickets. This was another of those moments. If any other man had shown such concern I would have immediately become defensive, telling him I could take care of myself. However, the fact that he was White seemed to give him a pass. I knew why but I still wasn't ready to admit it. At least not out loud.

Daylight came soon and the C.O. arranged for a van to take my partners and me to the nearest military airport. I asked where the rest of the men would go from here and White said most would stay behind to train and some would move onto other compounds. It was time to rearrange.

I'd been sitting in the sun for three days and was strongly aware of my lack of personal hygiene. This made me reluctant to sit near anyone on the flight back. Unfortunately I was paired up with Brown who smelled as bad as I did. Though I was eager to get back to my apartment and my shower, I was unable to stay awake during the flight. I only woke up because Brown elbowed me a good one after we landed.

"You snore," he grumbled.

"Only because you smell bad," I defended myself.

He laughed and told me he was only kidding, to which I replied, "I wasn't, you really do smell bad."

The chopper that normally resided on the top of White and Associates' office building was fueled and ready to go. We were all impatient to get home so we were in our seats before Brown was ready to lift off. I remained awake for the short flight home.

"We need to take our rifles back to the office," Blue told me as we exited the chopper.

It was a small side journey but I wished I could go straight to my apartment. I hadn't been home since I left to take the job at Gigi's.

Blue and I watched as the rest of the men got off the elevator one by one. Finally I heard one final ding signaling our arrival on the seventh floor. I followed Blue to the locked closet where we stored our prized possessions.

"I wanted to clean my rifle before putting her back into storage," I reluctantly handed him my case.

"Oh, I planned on cleaning them both tomorrow, if you don't mind."

"Sure. But, shouldn't I clean my own rifle?" His offer startled me.

"Yes, you should. But, I thought I'd help out," he shrugged his shoulders. "You've been working steadily for more than a month. Besides, we all got a check for the job you did for Colin."

"Okay. It'll be nice to have a day to myself, I guess." I appreciated the gesture. I knew he was trying to be nice so I wouldn't object, but it was awkward and a little personal to let him take care of my equipment.

"I promise I'll be careful," he gave me a knowing smile.

Blue and I made our way back to the elevator after he locked up our beauties. My mood lifted as we climbed ever closer to home. Blue exited before I did and I caught myself humming as the elevator opened up to my floor. I didn't even try to control the smile on my face as I walked toward my door.

I reached for my keys and realized I didn't have any. I'd given them to White the day Evans showed up to take me to Gigi's. Suddenly I was extremely self-conscious about my hygiene again. White had shown some interest for the first time in months and I didn't want to give him any reason to think I was repulsive.

I paced around outside my door for a few minutes before I decided to try Phil, the head of security for the building. He should have keys, I thought. Then I won't have to see White again until I'm cleaned up.

I rode the elevator back down to the lobby and found Phil at the main desk.

"Hi," I greeted him. He and I had a rocky past but after we both realized we were on the same team we'd become friends.

"Ms. Grey," he smiled. "How's it going?"

"Not too good, Phil. I don't have keys to my apartment and I was hoping you'd get me in."

"I'm sorry. I don't have keys for anything but the first floor here," he gestured with his hand. "Commander White is the only one with extra keys."

"Of course," I sighed. "Well, thanks anyway. I guess I'll talk to you later then."

He nodded his good-bye and I sulked back to the elevator. I pushed the button for White's floor but when the doors opened I stood motionless until they closed. I rode up to my apartment instead and double-checked, but my door was still locked and I still didn't have any keys.

What am I doing? I asked myself. This is stupid. It's not like he hasn't already seen me like this. I smoothed my hair. Why am I acting like this? I've known for years that I have a thing for White. Maybe I was finally ready to make that leap and accept his attentions. Maybe I'd make the first move. I giggled out loud and stepped back onto the elevator for the fourth time. I didn't know if I'd have the courage, but I decided when he handed me my keys I'd thank him with a kiss on the cheek. I started to sweat as I thought about his reaction and visibly jumped when the doors opened up to his apartment floor again.

Taking a deep breath I stepped out of the elevator and strode toward his door. My heart raced and I reminded myself I was just going to ask for my keys, unless he stood close enough. I suppressed the giggle wanting to escape.

I smoothed myself out again and knocked. The seconds seemed like years and he wasn't answering. I started to walk back to the elevator when I heard the door open. Turning toward the sound with a smile on my face I saw Judy Lacewell framing the doorway. We'd been involved in a few jobs for her, the most recent being the K&G job. K&G were contracted by the NSA for some jobs and had an embezzlement problem. I was sent in to search their computers to find the source. We all got in much deeper than expected.

My smile was instantly replaced with a grimace when I saw her. I didn't expect this at all. She had a past military history with my partners and made it very clear, by her attitude toward me, that I would never hold her respect.

"Can I help you," she asked, looking me up and down with disgust on her face.

"Uh," I stammered. "Is White available?" Her attitude annoyed me and made me even more self-conscious.

"He's in the shower," she hiked her head toward the bathroom. "I'll tell him you stopped by." The door shut and my stomach lurched.

I stood in shock, staring at the closed door. I thought Special Agent Lacewell and Red had a thing. However, I'd heard some stories about her. She didn't hide the fact that she liked men, all men. Any man. The word whore came to mind and then bitch. I considered knocking again and cracking her right in the mouth when she answered. I took a moment to think and decided against it because I didn't know why she was here.

With no hesitation this time I entered the elevator. As I rode it down I wondered what the hell I was going to do. I could hang out and wait until I saw Lacewell leave, but I needed a shower now. I could return to White's apartment when I thought he'd be done with his shower, but I didn't want to interrupt something else.

Again my stomach protested with that thought. So what if White got himself a girlfriend I told myself. I could get a boyfriend if I wanted one and he can't stop me, why would I be able to stop him. The elevator finally reached the lobby and I decided I didn't want to know what was going on in White's apartment.

I swept past Phil and he called after me, "Did you get into your apartment?"

"No, but that's okay," I called over my shoulder trying to keep my voice calm as I hurried toward the parking garage. The further I got from White's apartment, the further I got from my keys. The further I got from my keys the more enraged I became. Who did she think she was? Despite the fact I wanted to whack her a good one and yell at White because he let her act this way, I couldn't force myself back up to his apartment to try again.

Instead, I got behind the wheel of my puke green mustang. One thought dominated all others. What if White were dating her? I didn't know if I could ever forgive him. There was something about that woman, other than her lack of civility that made the hair on the back of my neck stand up.

Thank goodness my car had the uncanny ability to drive me to where I needed to be. I hadn't been to my parents' guesthouse for several months but it looked exactly the same as when I used to call it home. After a hurried shower I plopped on the couch and continued to brood. The what if's wouldn't leave me alone and before long I was convinced White and Lacewell were sharing more than the air in his apartment. This made me angrier than Lacewell dismissing me like she did. But he's been more attentive lately, I told myself. Why would he do that and have that floozy waiting for him in his apartment? Unless he wanted two for the price of one. I countered.

I'd been considering returning now that I'd had a shower but I couldn't go back to that apartment to ask for my keys with these thoughts in my head.

~~~~~~~~~~~~~~~~~~~~~~~~~~~~~~~~~~~~~

Cold and uncomfortable I rolled off the couch at three-thirty in the morning. I had been looking forward to curling up in my own bed. The soreness in my neck was really nagging at me. Standing near the couch I stretched and reached back to rub my neck. The darkness was thick but I knew the guesthouse well enough I made my way to the front door without incident.

I sighed inwardly when my hand touched the knob. I can just use extra blankets. It's not like I haven't slept through worse. I didn't even finish my thought before my anger returned. But I shouldn't have to! It's my apartment. I should be able to get in when I feel like it.

I was already in my car, speeding down the road before the vision of Lacewell reentered my mind. Though I'd convinced myself I didn't care, I didn't know if I could bear to see her in nothing but White's t-shirt. Not just that, if she shut the door in my face again, I'd have to smack her. I'll call ahead from the lobby. White shouldn't allow her to answer a call from his building security.

My excuse for not getting involved with White was because it could affect our working relationship. I couldn't let White's outside life affect me either. My job was more important than a fantasy. Besides, I could still have my fantasy even if White had an outside life.

I stopped in the lobby. Phil was absent but the guard manning the desk looked relieved to see me.

"Ms. Grey. Commander White told me to call as soon as you came in. He wanted me to tell you to wait here." The phone was already in his hands.

"Thanks," I said ungratefully. I suppose he didn't want me walking in on him and Lacewell. I felt nauseated.

After a brief conversation the guard told me White would be back in about half an hour.

"He said you could wait in his apartment if you'd like. He left it unlocked in case you came back."

"I'll wait here, thanks." I dropped heavily onto the nearest couch. I didn't want to admit it but I felt deflated. A couple of minutes ticked by as I sat there feeling sorry for myself. I'd planned on sitting peacefully on that couch until White arrived but soon found myself wandering around the highly polished black marble floor. I wanted to give up on White and the prospect of an "us" but I just couldn't yet. Maybe it would always remain a fantasy but I had to get past the manifestation of Lacewell into my little world. She didn't belong there and all I had to do was not think of her. My pacing around was making the guard uneasy so I made my way to the elevator.

"Can I tell White he'll find you in his apartment then?" His voice was unsettled.

"No. I'll be around." I was purposefully evasive. I'd worked myself up into a state of ill humor and was going to take every opportunity to be difficult.

"White will want to know where to find you when he gets back," the guard protested as the elevator doors shut.

I pressed every button so they couldn't go into the system to find out where I exited. It didn't take as long as I thought to reach the roof and I pressed all the buttons again as I stepped out.

I'd been to the roof a few times in the past to stare down at the city and had a favorite spot. I didn't go to that spot this time. Though it gave me a great view of the surrounding city the view didn't include the parking garage and I wanted to know the second White returned.

I was contemplating learning to hang glide when White's black Mustang tore into the garage. He was in a hurry.

"He better be," I said out loud. I'd been waiting all day for my keys. I had already decided to make him come look for me but knowing he was in the building and that he had my keys made me reconsider. I decided to appear without incident. The fact that I wanted to know exactly why Lacewell had been at his apartment influenced my decision a little. I pressed the button for the elevator.

I was greeted with a curious look from White when the doors opened. I'd expected to walk into an empty car and be given more time to collect my thoughts. Seeing White waiting for me threw me off guard but I recovered before he noticed.

"Keys?" I held out my hand.

"In my apartment," he held the elevator doors open with one hand and motioned me inside with the other.

I gave him an exasperated look and a loud sigh as I walked past him.

"Do you always have the lobby guard call to warn you when I show up?" I scoffed.

He wrinkled his forehead. "Phil called me as soon as you left. I almost caught you in the garage but you pulled out of here pretty fast. I've been waiting all day for you to come back to get your keys. We've got a job. And," he emphasized, "George Porter is missing. Where have you been?"

"Who?" I didn't know anyone named George Porter but White said it as if he were a good friend of mine.

"Mike Evans."

"What happened?" Before now, I didn't know Evans' real name. His disappearance came as a jolt. I hope I had nothing to do with this.

"We don't know where he's at. He could have left on his own accord or he could have been kidnapped or he could have been killed. That's why I've been out looking for you. You need to let me know where you are until this blows over," he lectured.

"I tried!" I didn't appreciate his fatherly tone. "That..." I wanted to say bitch but stopped myself and lowered my volume to normal. "I was here to get my keys once already. You're *girlfriend* answered the door. She told me you were in the shower and shut the door in my face." My nostrils flared. "I don't care what you do with your private life, but when I can't get the keys to *my* apartment because some woman doesn't want to be bothered, I get a little pissed off. I was tempted to knock again," I added, "but I didn't think violence was the answer." White was grinning.

"I don't find this the least bit funny." I glared viciously at him. "I haven't been to my apartment for more than a month and you think this is funny?" He was in dangerous territory now and he knew it. It wasn't just the fact I'd been deprived of my apartment but Evans vanishing was weighing on my mind.

"No, it's not funny and I'm sorry. I didn't know you'd been here and Lacewell was out of line." He let me into his apartment. "I'll speak with her. I'm just glad you're okay. I drove to your parent's house after I went past the Skylight but you weren't at either place. So, where were you?"

"It doesn't matter." I didn't mind being a little mysterious even if he probably missed me by only a few minutes. "When will we find out what happened to Evans, I mean Porter?"

"Take a seat," he motioned me toward the couch as he made his way to C.I.C. "There's quite a bit to tell." His voice was louder than it needed to be. "I left the paperwork in here." I started to get up to join him when he came back to the couch and handed me one of the large envelopes he held.

After we both got comfortable he continued. "We've got several irons in the fire right now."

"Don't we usually have more than one thing going on?"

"Yes. But three of our current jobs involve you in some way or another. Well, two of them and one other if you take it."

"We've got a job for Team Grey from DeLange. I'd like you to do the briefing since it'll be your team." White explained it was a retrieval of goods for the government. I continued to read and discovered the stolen goods were expected to be traded or sold near our Alaskan compound in three days. "Lacewell is the one who brought these jobs to us."

"I wouldn't want to disappoint your girlfriend." I used the word again to see if I could get him to admit or deny it.

"She," he began then changed his tenor. "Lacewell works for DeLange and he works for the Admiral and I wouldn't want to disappoint the Admiral. Your team is taking the job. I am asking you if you'd like to brief them."

"Yes, I'll do it."

"Good. The other job that could involve you comes from Lacewell. She wants us to see what we can find out about Evans' disappearance. I've got Red and Green on that one already."

"What am I supposed to do for that one?"

"Nothing. We are trying to figure out where Evans is but also want to find out if Emma Robertson is in any danger. That's how it involves you. The further away from this job you are the better. Then there is this," he handed me a separate, sealed manila envelope. "I also have a job for you, outside the company."

"What do you mean, outside the company?" I narrowed my eyes at him.

"White and Associates can not claim any connection to this job. Lacewell didn't have any information on it so I took the liberty of contacting the Admiral. It's for your eyes only."

I opened the envelope and noticed several bundles of cash in the bottom. I looked up at White who was watching me closely. I'd never been paid with cash up front before. This was not standard operating procedure so I started removing the paperwork. Pulling out a photo of Grigori I realized this would not be a test. Again I gave White a look. I was afraid I knew what this meant. I started removing the rest of the paperwork to find my objective. As I did this, a small slip of paper fluttered to the floor.

I bent to retrieve it and read the single word written on it.

"What's this?"

"This job comes with certain perks. You won't have to hack your Dad's password again."

"A password to the database?" I was mostly musing to myself.

"We are all still limited in what we can look up with our passwords so if there's more you want to know, you may still have to hack your Dad's password." He grinned.

"I can do that." I was so pleased with the password, the thoughts of the cash and my objective had moved to the back of my brain for a moment.

My little moment didn't last long as I continued to look through the paperwork. Grigori's specifics like his age, height and weight were listed. Another sheet showed a younger man. Airman Drummond was of slight build and had a dull look to his eyes. Airman. He was Air Force. I didn't know about this.

"Did you go through this?" I indicated the envelope.

"No. I won't either. The decision is yours to make. However, I've been given a few details. I know where and when this is to take place."

I kept going through the packet and found my objective. A stark white sheet of paper simply read:

*Elimination of targets and all associates at assigned location.*

"You've been hired outside of White and Associates but we will be working in concert with you on this one," White interrupted my reading.

"How can we work together if no one is to know about my involvement," I was dubious.

"I'm sure you have at least one target to take down." I nodded. "This mission coincides with the job I want you to debrief your team for. When you have completed your mission, Team Grey will move in, mop up and recover the goods. Your presence will be explained by your briefing. No one but I will know about your side job and no one can ever know about it. Is that understood?"

"Yes," I said with a lump in my throat.

"So, do you accept?"

All of a sudden this felt like my first job I'd ever done. I knew we could never be associated with the government and they would never claim hiring White & Associates, but for White to tell me that he and my partners wouldn't claim this job was almost a slap in the face. If it weren't for the eager look White had I would have refused on that basis alone.

It took me a few seconds to wrap my head around it all but I made my decision.

"Yes. I accept." I replied and the lump moved from my throat into the pit of my stomach. "However, this is an unprepared acceptance and I may change my mind. I want to do a little research first."

White told me to make it quick and meet him in the office by six. This gave me less than an hour to do any research so I hurriedly took my keys he dug from a kitchen drawer.

I'd been aching to get back to the world of technology so I went directly to my computer and tried out my password. Sure enough, I was granted access to the government database. First things first, I told myself, resisting the urge to test my limits.

I looked up Airman Drummond and was rewarded with his service record as well as the current investigation on him. He'd been caught stealing weapons but had eluded arrest. The details of his escape were nothing special. He knew he was under investigation and quietly disappeared before the investigation was complete. It was later discovered, because of the bug I'd planted in Dimitri's office, that Drummond was to make an exchange with Grigori. I was hired to put a stop to this transfer but my name wasn't listed and neither was White and Associates.

A familiar name caught my eye as I skimmed the transcript of what the bug captured. With the recognition of this name my mind was made up. If I didn't do this it wouldn't only affect our government negatively, it could possibly affect White and Associates. I realized at that very moment where my loyalties were. I was fiercely proud of my government, but if White and Associates were hurt in anyway, life as I knew it, would end.

With my decision firm I took a few minutes to search around the database a little more. I wanted to see what kind of information I'd be restricted from so I did some general searches. The access denied screen didn't rear it's ugly head with any of my searches so I purposefully started searching things I knew would be restricted, even to my father, and I was granted full access to everything.

I looked over my shoulder, expecting to be busted by the computer police. This was too much for me to be trusted with. What was I going to do? This could be fun, but I knew I'd better let my dad know what kind of access he'd given me. I toyed with the idea of calling him immediately but decided I'd wait. Having this kind of access could be helpful, not to mention fun.

After I searched around a little more I packed only what I needed. I included my .50 cal. when I reached the office. I did a quick inspection and was happy with the job Blue had done on it. I double-checked everything to make sure I wasn't being duped again into thinking this was a real mission when it was training and was disappointed to find nothing was out of place. This was real.

The flight to the compound didn't take long enough. Before I was ready, I found myself briefing my team. White stood at my side at attention, making me a little uncomfortable. When I finished the briefing he led the team out the door to prepare for tomorrow's action and I made my way to my quarters.

# Chapter Eleven

White came to my door and found me ready to go. He told me the men were still making their preparations. He'd told them we were going to go scout the area in the chopper.

"You're quiet," White noticed when we were more than fifteen minutes out.

"Thinking," I lied. My brain had shut itself off and I was in a stupor. I was watching a movie with myself as the main character and no matter how loudly I screamed at the screen the actor just couldn't hear me. I was following a script that I could not deviate from.

"Well, your team has a sniper, too, so you have to make sure you aren't seen or leave a trail to be found. When we get closer I'll describe the playing field a little more."

He did just that as we flew over the designated area. I already knew where I was going to spend the night. I knew it was going to be cold and miserable but I'd accepted the job.

White set the chopper down and I jumped out and headed for my hiding spot.

"Good luck!" I heard him say as I moved away but I didn't look back.

I made my way to my chosen place of concealment and I checked the surroundings with my scope. The only movement were the waves on the Arctic Ocean. The air was brisk and intensely quiet. This only added to my dreamlike state. Eventually I settled in for the night and my uncanny calm settled in deeper. My brain started to allow thoughts a few hours into the mission. However, my thoughts weren't filled with any emotion at all.

As expected, the night was bitter and I rubbed my hands together wondering how long my gloves could stand the friction. With the morning light came the sound of a chopper from somewhere behind me. I tensed. I knew the drop would occur before my team arrived and was anxious to get this over with.

The chopper set down and three men exited. I didn't move my eye from my sight. A boat came near the shore and the men standing near the chopper started to unload several crates.

Grigori was stepping out of the boat with two other men. The three of them made their way toward the boxes. I saw one of Grigori's men bend down and open all of the crates.

They were full of weapons. I steadied myself and considered the man who was receiving a briefcase from Grigori. I'd only seen the back of his head and didn't realize he'd be familiar as well. My brain still wouldn't allow me to think emotionally. I personally knew some of the men I was sent to kill but it didn't affect me like I thought it should. They were the ones selling the contraband, after all. I knew I'd be able to take all six of them, but I needed to get them in a particular order to throw everyone off.

Grigori would be first. I felt the kick of my gun and chambered the next round. Next, I took out one of the men who'd come with Grigori. By now, the four left standing had their guns trained on each other and were all talking at the same time.

I pulled the trigger again, dropping one of the men I once knew. Again, I felt the kick of the weapon and saw another body drop. The two remaining men were running for the boat but fell to the ground in a heap before they made it halfway there. I surveyed the scene with a clinical aloofness. Every man who'd stepped foot on that shore that morning, would remain there.

I stood from my hiding spot and pushed the button on my GPS watch. This was the signal to set my team to its task. I'd meet White elsewhere for retrieval.

I hiked out with my self-awareness slowly returning. The stillness was no longer there and I started to bawl. I knew two of those men out there and I'd taken their lives. They were running guns I reminded myself and the crying stopped. I analyzed my feelings and my emotion didn't come from killing any of the six men. It was a release of energy I'd been suppressing. Instead, I used this energy to get myself to the extraction point.

White was waiting on a lake with the plane instead of the chopper.

"And?" White asked as I strapped in.

"And, it's done."

A small group from Team Grey had left the compound in Jeeps as soon as White received my GPS transmission and were just arriving on scene. White was receiving the operations transmissions and handed me a headset of my own.

"I see six down and no movement. Proceed with caution," I heard someone say. White gave me a questioning look.

After a short time I heard someone else say, "All clear. Grab the merchandise, men." Then, from the same voice, "Shit! It's Johns." I watched the color drain from White's face as he turned to look at me.

I gave him a slow nod and added, "and Sullivan."

"Sealed envelope is in place. Let's move!" The urgency in the man's voice reminded me I'd killed my own men.

"I brought you a change of clothes." White motioned to a duffle bag in the back.

"Keep your eyes forward," I ordered as I started to undress. White complied and didn't steal any peeks when I was watching.

We set down on the lake of our compound just as I was stuffing my used garb back into the bag. White took it from me and exited the plane. I carried my rifle back to my room with White trailing behind me.

"What the hell went on out there?" he asked as soon as we were inside my room with the door shut.

"I did my job," I didn't feel like talking about it.

"Johns?"

"Yes, and Sullivan." I shrugged my shoulders. I wouldn't allow him to make me feel guilty for a job he'd brought to me.

"I didn't see this coming. What do I tell the men? Johns was demoted but he was still stationed here."

"Let's get down to C.I.C. and follow this to the end."

---

"Stevens." He was sitting at a computer.

"Commander," he had a sick look on his face.

"Where are the men?" I asked.

"About an hour out yet, Ma'am."

"I hear Johns was among the dead?" I feigned innocence.

"Yes, Ma'am."

"Well, he was one of us. We need to find out what was going on out there. Even if the client doesn't want us to know." I knew I'd done the right thing, but knew there'd be questions. "White, you go talk to the C.O. and find out everything you can about Johns and Sullivan, Stevens and I will work from here."

I took a seat at a computer screen and punched in my unrestricted password. I pulled up the same information I'd found before and printed out the relevant pieces.

After White returned I handed him the paperwork.

"What did you find out?" I asked before he could look at the information in his hands. He told me the C.O. had given Johns a week of R&R and he wasn't due back until tomorrow. "No one has seen or heard from Sullivan, since we fired him."

I allowed White to read what Johns and Sullivan had been up to and waited for him to begin the conversation again.

He took me aside so Stevens couldn't hear our conversation then started, "You knew, didn't you."

"Of course I did. What I don't know is, how do we explain this to the men?"

"I think we can give them a brief version to allay their concerns."

The men returned at the expected time. During the debriefing, White made it clear, the only reason the men were privy to any of this information was for morale purposes and because of the proximity to the company. He then went on to tell them that we'd been sent out to clean up a gun deal gone wrong.

The condensed version of what they witnessed visibly helped the men and they all walked out of C.I.C. with a load off their shoulders.

When they were all gone, White handed me the briefcase they'd recovered and said, "Here's the remainder of your payment, less twenty-five percent for the company, of course."

I didn't expect this and my mouth dropped open. I considered refusing, but decided against it. I didn't know how much was in the case but wondered how I'd claim it on my taxes.

---

White and I returned to the office the next day and I went straight to my apartment. I didn't want to be around people and reluctantly answered my door when I saw Colin through the peephole.

"I've come to see how you're doing," he admitted as I let him in.

"I'm fine. Why wouldn't I be?"

"Well, Porter's disappearance for one thing and now this other thing your team was involved in..." Colin hesitated, a look of empathy on his face.

"I'm sorry men from the company were involved. I know hearing about their deaths can't be easy for you. White informed me that all the participants were already dead when your team arrived. At least they weren't met with enemy fire. I've got a team of my own already en-route to 'discover' the bodies. It's probably a good thing you didn't go out with the team." I knew Colin had hired my team for the retrieval so I'd assumed he knew about my outside job. Now I wondered.

His sympathetic speech made me raise my eyebrows. He thought I couldn't handle seeing dead people. I knew he'd hired my team for retrieval but he had no knowledge or my job.

"Colin, I'm fine." I put my hands on my hips for emphasis. "I don't think I ever told you this but, I've killed before. That's sometimes a part of my job. And, I've even had a price on my head by one of the richest men in the world." My voice was callous as I referred to a side effect of the K&G job I was sure he was aware of.

But I wanted him to understand I could hold my own in any situation. His pity was misplaced and just flat pissed me off.

"What? You never told me you'd killed someone. Why didn't you tell me?" He was shocked.

"Didn't think it was something to brag about. Plus, I didn't want you to think of me differently. But, I don't like you thinking I can't cope with *everything* my job might bring my way." By now, my brow was furrowed in anger.

"I know you're right, Alex. I knew what this company did when you took the job. I didn't really consider you being put into these kinds of positions and I'll just have to get used to it. I presumed they'd keep you closer to home with your jobs. Utilize your computer skills and keep you safer."

"I don't care if you ever get used to the idea of me doing what I do. I love this job." We were quiet long enough for me to get even more worked up. "I take that back about not caring if you get used to it or not. You better get used to it if you are going to take the Admiral's place and wish to use the company. If you request I'm not used in any mission because you are afraid I might get hurt, you'll be the one getting hurt." I was furious but Colin found my diatribe funny.

"I know. I think I needed this ass chewing to remind me of how capable you really are." He knew I was fuming and tried to calm me down with a rub to my arm. I pulled away which surprised him. "Alex, I'm trying to apologize here. You are my best friend and I don't want to ever lose you, especially to something I've done."

I quieted my attitude. "I understand, Colin. But, we have each made our own decisions and we have to live with whatever they bring."

We changed the subject and tried to catch up. Our conversation remained strained until Colin left. Before now, I'd never found myself wishing Colin wasn't in the same room with me. When he finally did leave, I felt relieved but empty.

Over the next hour I sat on my couch, feeling sorry for myself, *again*. Colin had no faith in me, White had a girlfriend, had me killing people, and I felt fat. When I caught myself standing in front of my bathroom mirror with my shirt raised I knew I was being stupid.

Colin was trying to protect me and White was just being a man trying to further my career. I guess I don't mind Colin's concern. It was sweet. As for White's girlfriend, it was none of my business unless I chose to express my feelings and then, only if he felt the same. His job choices for me were much more important right now than his bed partners. I decided to really think about what I'd done. I'd killed six men, two of whom I'd actually had conversations with.   But, I didn't feel any real loss other than my innocence.

I put my shoes on and ended up driving around.   Somehow I ended up in my parent's driveway.   I went with the flow and spent the evening talking with my mother about my sniper training.   I wanted to tell her about my recent job but knew I couldn't tell anyone, though she probably already knew.   One of my main concerns I expressed to her was actually killing and how to get past it.   I thought if anyone would know what I was going through, she would.   I wasn't disappointed and returned to my apartment feeling much better.

# Chapter Twelve

White was waiting in the lobby when I returned and he rode the elevator up with me.

"I told you I need to know where you are at all times until we find out about Evans," he scolded.

"I had some thinking to do and I didn't know where I was going or when I'd be back." I actually liked the attention from White but I didn't like the restrictions so my tone was defiant.

"I know you don't like this," he started.

"Do you hover like this when it happens to another partner?" I interrupted.

"That's just the thing. It doesn't happen. There's something about you that just," he paused, "draws attention."

I stepped off the elevator at my floor and he followed me. This I didn't expect.

"I suppose you want to come in," I said rudely. I wanted nothing more than to spend time with him but I couldn't get Lacewell out of my head.

"I don't have to come in." White was clearly stunned at my remark.

"I'm sorry. Of course you can come in." I reminded myself that his choice of lovers was of no relevance to our working relationship or friendship. We entered my apartment and he went immediately to my couch and made himself at home. My clothes from the Emma Robertson job were still in the suitcases and I decided to take the time to put them away.

"Would you make some coffee?" I asked as I carried a suitcase to my bedroom.

"Sure," he replied from the kitchen as I opened the case. The phone I'd been given was on top of the clothes and blinking. I had a message.

"White?" I held the phone out in front of myself as I walked toward the kitchen.

"What's this?" He gave me a curious look.

"Emma's phone and there are several messages."

"Who is it?"

"It must be Evans."

After pushing some buttons White put the phone to his ear. I watched his face for any hints about the message. He only listened to a couple of the messages and didn't reveal anything until he hung up and called Red from his own phone. He gave Red the address of the apartment I used as Emma and told him to check it out with extreme caution and get back with him right away.

"It was Evans?" I thought I already knew the answer.

"No. It was someone named Sal. Said he had Evans and would keep him until you showed up."

My mouth went dry as I thought about Evans and the message. Sal had been a zealous flirt but I didn't think he would have done anything like this. I hoped Red and Green would find Evans and bring him back. I felt guilty for not having the phone on me.

White must have read my expression and told me I couldn't have known this was going to happen.

I went back to putting my clothes away while we waited for Red to call back. For some reason it felt like he might call sooner if I just got these clothes out of the way. I quickly finished the job and Red still hadn't called.

"Maybe you should call him back."

"No. He'll call. Be patient."

White and I sat on the couch sipping our coffee for what seemed like an eternity. I watched my feet for a bit and then moved my gaze to White's boots. I studied them for a while before I realized how close they were to my own. I immediately felt restless. If White were really seeing Lacewell I felt uncomfortable sitting this close to him. Especially since I felt the way I did about him. I'd resolved to dislike Lacewell but if White liked her I wouldn't want to do anything to disrupt his happiness. As my mind raced with thoughts like this my eyes were slowly making observations of White's feet, legs, and finally his arm before his phone rang. My eyes jumped to his and he was watching me inquisitively. Time stopped. The phone rang again before his eyes left mine. I was breathless. White had given me all kinds of looks but nothing ever so potently amorous. He hung up after a couple of affirmative answers to quick questions and one "Yes, Grey's apartment." I was still unsettled by the few seconds our eyes had locked and I didn't trust my voice to ask him who it was. Instead I adverted my eyes and rose to get coffee. I didn't know if the look was calculated on his part and was afraid to ask.

Neither of us spoke as I brought the pot over to give White a refill. While I put the pot back on the burner there was a knock at my door. My mind was aflutter with thoughts of White as I headed toward the door to answer it.

"I've got it," I noticed White rise to answer it himself.

When I opened the door it was like being slapped in the face. Lacewell tried to walk past me into my apartment as if I weren't even at the door.

"I'm here to see White." Her tone was full of disdain and contempt when I stood in her way.

I didn't reply. Instead I looked her up and down like she'd done to me and shut the door in her face.

"What did you do that for?" White was asking as Lacewell knocked insistently on my door.

"If you let her into my apartment I'll punch you right in the mouth." I growled, standing in front of my door with my hands balled into tight fists.

"Are you serious?"

"You're damn right I'm serious." Lacewell's incessant beating on my door had stopped and White's phone rang.

"Just hold on, Lacewell," White sounded exasperated tone. "Alex, you have to let her in. She's here because of Evans."

I surrendered and relaxed my clenched hands. White started to reach past me for the doorknob. He stopped when he was close enough I could have heard his heartbeat if I'd have held my breath. He faltered, his arm falling back to his side. He sighed loudly and said, "Okay." Lifting his phone back to his ear he then said, "Just meet us at the office," then he hung up.

I walked past him, retrieved my coffee from the kitchen then made my way back to the couch. I had no intentions of going to meet with Lacewell.

"We'll give her a chance to stand there for a while before we go down." White joined me.

"Why?" I had to know why.

"She pisses me off a lot, too," he shrugged.

"But, shouldn't you take her side in this?"

"Was she right?"

"No," of that I was sure.

"Then, no."

"Won't this get you into trouble?" I loved the fact that he was taking my side but couldn't help but prod. I wanted to make sure he and Lacewell weren't a couple.

White narrowed his eyes at me as a devilish grin spread across his face. "In trouble with whom?"

"*Her.*"

"I suppose, to some extent." The grin was still there. He added, "We better get down there before Red calls. This is very unprofessional."

I nodded and got to my feet. Though I hadn't planned on going to the office I had to see their reactions to each other. I hadn't gotten any information from him and his villainous grin had confused me. Did he know I was pushing for information or was he smiling like that for another reason?

We rode the elevator down in silence and I led the way into the office. Lacewell was sitting in Gabriella's chair when I walked in. She stood and gave me a cross look. I happily returned the expression.

"Okay, ladies," White stepped between us to get our attention. "We will be working together so we need to build a good rapport. First of all, Lacewell," he directed all of his attention to her. "When you are at my apartment for business, or any other reason, you will treat my guests with respect. If I hear that you've turned anyone away again without informing me that I have company, we will have to do all our business dealings here at the office. Am I understood?"

She rolled her eyes, said, "Yes," but gave a loud sigh as if his requirements were ludicrous.

"Ms. Grey." Now he turned to me. "I completely understand why you don't want Lacewell in your apartment after the way she treated you. However, I expect you to treat our *other* clients appropriately."

I was expecting him to reprimand me like he did Lacewell, but instead, he gave me permission to dislike her. I nodded my agreement and held my head higher as he led the way into his office.

The stillness between the three of us would have been more than I could bear if Red hadn't called almost as soon as we sat down.

White's conversation was short and his expression troubled as he handed the phone to Lacewell.

"That was Red," White told me as Lacewell spoke on the phone. "They found him." His voice was muted so I worried if Evans was still alive.

"Just go in and get him!" Lacewell yelled to Red.

"We've got to go," White said to me. "According to your messages, Sal wants Emma, so you are going to go get Evans back for us. Lacewell, let's go." She was totally absorbed with her phone call but managed to follow us to White's Mustang in the parking garage.

She got into the backseat without hesitation, allowing me to ride shotgun.

White handed me Emma's phone as we were driving.

"Call him and tell him you just got the messages. He still thinks you are Emma so you will be."

Sal picked up on the first ring.

"Emma?"

"Yes," I had a tremble in my voice.

"Did you get my messages?" He sounded eager.

"Yes. You didn't hurt Mr. Evans did you?"

"No. Here, you can talk to him." There was a short pause and then I heard Evans voice.

"Emma?"

"Are you okay?"

"Yes. Where are you?" He replied.

"Almost there. Is he well armed?"

I heard some rustling and then Sal's voice.

"Where is she?" When Evans didn't answer quickly enough, "Where are you?"

"I'm almost home."

"Are you alone?"

"Yes."

His tone turned ominous. "You better hurry. I've been waiting for you for a long time. Where did you go?" He didn't give me the chance to reply before he fired off another question and another.

White stopped a block from the apartment and told me to walk the rest of the way and keep him on the phone. I did as I was told and saw Sal watching from my apartment window. As soon as he saw me his questions stopped.

"Hurry up," he said.

I picked up my pace and walked straight for the apartment. I looked around as I crossed the street, hoping to see Red and Green somewhere nearby.

Just as I noticed them sitting in a car near my apartment, Sal said, "What are you looking for?"

"I'm just watching for cars while I cross the street," I lied.

"Well, don't." He hung up.

White drove past me at a normal pace and I watched as he parked down the street out of sight of the apartment. I didn't know how this was going to pan out. I'd never had a stalker before. If only I had realized how unstable Sal was while I was at Gigi's I could have taken precautions.

Sal was waiting with the door open.

"Get in here," he waved a gun at me.

"Okay, just relax."

I saw Evans tied up in the corner as soon as I walked in so I started to make my way to him.

"Leave him alone. I want to know where you were," Sal demanded.

"I told you she was back home, tying up some loose ends."

"I didn't ask you, old man." Sal pointed the gun at Evans threateningly. He turned his attention back to me. "You didn't tell anyone where you were going, you just left."

"I couldn't work at Gigi's anymore. They were going to make me dance and I just couldn't do that, Sal." I was improvising.

"Why? You would have been the best dancer there."

"I didn't want to take my clothes off in front of strangers." He stood, thinking.

"Well, that's good, I guess," he said finally.

"Give me the gun, Sal." I reached for it and thought he was going to give it to me until he grabbed my arm and pulled me toward him.

"I don't think so. I need to deal with him first." While holding me in a chokehold with one arm he waved the gun toward Evans. I struggled against him but realized he had a better hold on me than I'd previously thought.

He fired the gun and I tried to pull free at the same time. Evans slumped to the floor and blood slowly pooled around him. My phone rang inside my pocket. Sal kept his grip on me and slowly turned me toward him. My phone rang again.

"Answer it and tell them not to come in," he ordered.

"Who? I came alone," I lied.

"I'm not dumb! Just do it," he shook the pistol at me.

"Yes?" I tried to sound calm.

"What happened? We're coming in." White's voice was intense.

"Not a good idea." Sal took my phone from me and hung it up.

"You are damn good looking but not that good looking. We found the bug you planted."

"What do you mean?" I continued to try to play Emma.

"Don't even..." he let his sentence die. "You were the only girl who up and left, making you the prime suspect. I know for sure now because of all your friends outside." He shoved the gun into my gut making me double over.

"We are leaving now." He wrenched me around, holding my arm behind my back. Pushing me toward the door he told me, "Open it, slowly, and walk out, slowly." As soon as the door was opened it revealed Red standing there. His sidearm aimed at us.

"Take it easy," he said as Sal pulled me closer to him, his arm back around my throat.

"Back off," Sal said as he pushed the gun to my temple.

Red holstered his gun and backed away. "Lets talk about this. She's just a woman. You don't want to do this for a woman."

I started to shake my head, knowing that Sal knew I wasn't who I claimed to be. He pushed the gun harder against my head, preventing me from moving any more.

"I'm not stupid. What are you guys? F.B.I.? It doesn't matter, I'm walking out of here. Back off!" Sal was getting jumpy.

"Evans," I croaked but my air was cut off by Sal's arm.

"Move it!" He kept his back against the wall as he moved toward the parking lot. Red stepped into the apartment as we moved further away.

Sal slowly pulled me to the parking lot. I tried to look around but couldn't move my head. I couldn't see anyone else and started to feel a panic rising. I couldn't let him get me into a vehicle. I tried to struggle but he just solidified his grip around my neck cutting off all of my air. I planted my feet and he tried to move me onward but failed until he lifted me by my neck. Grabbing hold of his arm with both my hands, I tried to lift myself up some so I could breathe. I failed and his grip only got stronger.

We reached a dark colored Jeep and he put me back down on my feet but didn't loosen his grip. My head started to swim and I felt weak. I fought against it but knew if he didn't ease up I was going to pass out. I felt him trying to fish his keys from his pocket but my vision was failing. My legs faltered and I went limp, sliding out of his grip. I had the sensation of falling but didn't feel anything when I hit the ground.

The next thing I knew White was kneeling beside me, brushing my hair out of my face. My stomach was turning and my head hurt.

"Come on, wake up," he coaxed gently. "We got him," he said when I opened my eyes.

I tried to apologize for passing out but my throat hurt and nothing came out.

"We're lucky he cut off your air. It gave us a chance to take him down." His voice was soothing and despite my humiliation I felt somewhat better until I saw Lacewell standing in the background, grinning.

I managed to partially sit up. In spite of my sore throat, I asked about Evans.

"He'll be okay, because of you." This time it was Lacewell. Her tone was grateful, but strained. "He was shot in the shoulder and just played dead. He said that your struggling with Sal must have made him miss his mark."

"Sal knew I'd planted the bug," I told White.

"You were out for a couple of minutes.  We know all this already and have it under control."

"What?" I was confused.

"Emma Robertson and Michael Evans were killed here today but not before taking out the gunman."

"Sal's dead?"

"No, but he'll be detained.  Probably indefinitely." Green added as he joined us.

"The ambulance is on its way," Red informed White.

"You and I will ride in the ambulance with Evans and you'll both die at the hospital, so don't look too well yet." White told me.

I gratefully laid back down and didn't hide how I really felt. I was sore all over and it was easier to look miserable than not to.

# Chapter Thirteen

Black and I went to the cabin right after Emma was admitted to the hospital. They all agreed it would be good for me to stay out of the city for a while.

"Besides," White told me when I objected, "you're up for a little vacation time."

After some half-hearted complaints I finally agreed to go to the cabin. I always found myself yearning for it anyway, especially now that they'd rebuilt it and added some real technology to the place.

White had driven Black and me to the drop off point so we could hike the distance. We'd been given the option to be dropped off by Brown in the chopper but both of us wanted to do the long hike again. My first time up we'd broken everyone's record for hiking time to the cabin and wanted to retest ourselves.

Unfortunately we didn't press as hard as we should have and instead of one day it took us three to reach the cabin. I was the first one to leave the designated route to do a little exploring but Black soon found something off the trail he wanted to see and we hiked around in circles.

Sleeping out in the open is always invigorating but I was thankful to be at the cabin for our third night. My bed was more comfortable than the ground.

Black and I didn't waste any time and spent almost every waking hour outside. We went cave diving the first day. I'd forgotten how beautiful and awesome the caves under the lake were. The caverns snaked all through the mountains around us but one passage led into the basement of the cabin.

Over the next couple of weeks we went base-jumping, did a lot of hiking and even did some target practice. Black never missed an opportunity to teach me something and had decided I needed to be proficient in archery. Every day, before we did anything else, I'd take the bow and arrows out to the range and practice. Black had shown me how to hold the bow and draw back the string properly but I still seemed to whack myself every so often. I had big welts that turned to bruises on my arm. It hurt more each time I did it and I found myself swearing loudly when I let my arm get in the way of the bowstring.

"Language." Black criticized.

"Sorry," I replied. Men, I thought to myself. They can swear and be thought macho but when I do it I'm considered uncivil. Instead of swearing I began to stomp my foot and hold my breath until the pain eased up. After one of my stomping sessions I noticed Black grinning while he let an arrow fly so I decided not to make any show of being affected.

Finally, after two weeks of wonderful weather a thunderstorm kicked up so we spent the day in the cabin. I considered going up to the library and poking around on the computers but found a book instead.

At dinner Black asked if I'd like to go on a camping trip. He laid out a large map across the table.

"I've never been here, or here," he pointed to different locations on the map.

"Neither have I," I grinned at him. I'd been to various places near the cabin but it was mostly for training purposes. I hadn't been allowed the time to do much exploring. Black smiled back at me and we continued to pick our route on the map.

Before the sun made an appearance we were already miles from the cabin. The rain from the previous day hadn't dried up and I was soaked and shivering when we took a breakfast break.

"Did you bring extra clothes?" Black asked.

"Of course," I was surprised he asked.

"I'll wait for you to change."

"That's okay. The sun is coming out. I should dry up soon."

"Have it your way," he raised his eyebrows.

After the sun lit the world we slowed our pace and enjoyed the scenes around us. But when the sun went down we picked up our pace again and hiked through the night. I hadn't expected this and by the time the sun rose on the second day I was decidedly tired. Again, we slowed our pace until the sun went down. We continued this way for the first three days but on the third night, Black said we were going to set up camp.

"We're getting out of familiar territory," he explained.

I didn't care what his reasons were. I was thrilled we were stopping for the night.

I laid out my bedroll and was inside before Black had his ready. I contemplated how comfortable the ground was this far from the cabin for only a few seconds before I fell asleep. I didn't wake up until the sun was far above the horizon.

Looking around for Black I found him near my bedroll. He was still wrapped up and snoring quietly. I was shocked to be up before him.

I cleaned up my bedroll as quietly as I could. Then I went to Black's backpack for the map. I opened it up a short distance from the still sleeping Black so the rustling wouldn't disturb him.

We'd made good time and should be at our destination in less than an hour. The closeness of our goal made me wonder how long Black was going to sleep.

I started a fire to make breakfast and Black's head peeked out from inside his bed.

"I'm getting old," he said as he realized the time.

I smiled but didn't say anything. I didn't think he was getting old but Black and I communicated mostly without words. Well, Black rarely communicated with words.

As I suspected, we were at our destination within an hour after breakfast and we weren't disappointed. The color green was everywhere and the air smelled of fresh rain.

The scene was like a jungle with close vegetation around a clear stream. Black's target had been a small pond created by the stream. The sun filtered in through the moss-covered trees perfectly and I found myself wishing I'd brought a camera. Black already had one out and was looking mighty professional walking around taking shots.

We spent two days camped near the pool. All the while Black was taking pictures of the area. The night before we started our grueling trek back to the cabin I found out Black was an aspiring photographer. He promised to show me some of his work when we returned to the cabin.

We didn't slow our pace for our return trip and made it back to the cabin in less time than it took to get to the small, secluded pond. Again, I was tired from the strenuous hike and lack of sleep. I planned on taking a shower and going straight to bed, but as we neared the cabin we realized there was someone there.

Lights shined through the windows so we slowed our pace. As we neared the cabin we both made an attempt to make no noise. Black motioned me around the back of the cabin while he made his way to the kitchen window.

I was nearing the back door when I heard Black say, "It's clear." I turned and walked back toward him. Inside I saw Brown and White at the table.

"Wonder what's going on? We aren't due to go back for a few days." I said as we walked toward the front door.

"Let's find out." He opened the front door and stepped in.

I heard White's voice. "Have you two had dinner?"

"Not yet," Black replied as we set our packs down.

"Long day?" Brown alluded to my appearance.

"Long week." Black answered for me.

"You're here early. What's up?" I couldn't stand not knowing.

"Nothing. Just thought we'd come up and relax for a couple of days." White said.

We stayed near the cabin for the next two days. Black suggested I keep up on my archery practice every morning so my healing bruises became fresh bruises. For some reason, I couldn't remember to keep my arm out of the way of the bowstring.

"You're holding it all wrong," White had snuck up behind me and I jumped at his voice.

"You scared me." I couldn't help but smile.

"You need to pay more attention to your surroundings at all times," his eyebrows went up to compliment his sinister grin. He walked toward me and stood uncomfortably close. He wrapped his arms around me from behind, gripping the bow through my hands. I tried to take slow, deep breaths to keep myself from shaking at his touch but this only worsened matters. His scent was even more intoxicating than his touch. Purposefully I took some breaths through my mouth and calmed myself. His embrace was strong and solid, making me feel protected and vulnerable at the same time.

"I'm never going to remember this," I muttered.

"Yes, you will," he answered my unintentional utterance by turning me toward him.

He gave me the same smoldering look he'd given me in my apartment the day we were waiting for Red to call back with news of Evans. I got lost in the moment and again time seemed to stand still. Slowly his face came closer to mine and this time I wouldn't stop him. I wasn't ready but had come to the conclusion that I'd never be ready for White. It was time to let him take the lead.

"Hey," Black's voice was sharp in our ears, making us both jump. White slowly let his grip loosen and we turned to face the unwanted interruption.

"This is practice time." Black tried, but couldn't fully hide the smile on his face.

"You didn't show her how to hold the bow correctly," White accused with no hint of the embarrassment I felt.

"Then, by all means," Black gestured toward the bow.

My composure had left me and I was visibly shaking when White regained his grip.

"I can't do this now."

"It's okay. Take a deep breath and forget everything else until he leaves," his voice was low in my ear, making it impossible to forget his advance or Black's presence. I closed my eyes and let White use my arms to pull back the bowstring. He told me to keep my arms close to his and I felt him release the arrow and didn't feel the burning of the string on my arm.

"Now, try it on your own," he backed away.

I readied the bow and stood shaking while I sited in the arrow. I closed my eyes and remembered White's hold and let my arms move to the proper place. After I opened my eyes again I made sure my arrow was still heading in the right direction and let it fly. Again, the bowstring didn't touch my arm.

"You see," White directed at Black. "You're methods are faulty."

"You could be right," Black turned and left us alone, the smile still lingering at the edges of his mouth.

"That's two for two," White said when Black was out of earshot. I had made my way to a lone hay bale and plopped down, my energy gone.

White joined me and we sat in silence until I quit shaking.

"You should practice some more," he stood and held out his hand.

I took it and gave him a grateful smile. The moment was gone, though the after effects still remained. He shrugged his shoulders as if he knew exactly what was going through my mind.

I didn't have any more trouble with the bowstring as long as I visualized White behind me, holding my arms. This vision interfered with my accuracy but at least I wasn't going to be bruised.

White and I retrieved the arrows I'd shot all around the target and started back to the cabin.

"I wonder who's paid him to be the protector of your virtue," White said as we walked.

"He's good at it." I gave a weak smile.

After reaching the cabin we all packed up our things and started getting the cabin ready for our absence. I picked tasks that kept me away from White and Black. I didn't want to talk about what had almost happened with either of them. I suspected Black wouldn't mention anything but didn't want to take any chances.

Before long I found myself with nothing to do so I went for a walk down to the lake where I passed several hours walking along the shore. Brown came looking for me after the sun had disappeared behind the mountains.

"Supper's about ready. Not that you need it," he teased.

"Okay," I walked toward him.

"What's going on?" He asked when I reached his side.

"What do you mean?"

"Black and White had an argument about something and you've been invisible," his tone was curious.

"I don't know what's going on with those two but I've been out here because I'm going to miss it."

"Yeah, I'm not buying it."

"Fine by me."

"See, you aren't even fighting with me."  He stopped in the middle of the trail.

I reached out and smacked his head and bolted for the cabin.

"See!  That's more like it," I heard his voice close behind me so I picked up my pace.

I felt more like myself at dinner but things were obviously strained between Black and White until Brown and I got involved in a small food fight.

"You two are on kitchen duty tonight," Black ordered.

Brown quickly stood from the table and saluted Black, "Yes, sir!"

This made us all grin, except Black.  He stood from the table with a serious look.  Then when Brown and White weren't looking he gave me a wink.

This prompted me to get up and start cleaning up our mess. Brown was still in rigid formation but relaxed his stance and began to help me.  We hadn't made much of a mess so the clean up wasn't too bad.

"My job here is done," Brown said when we finished.  "I'm going to bed, we have an early day tomorrow."

After Brown and Black were safely in their rooms White asked me if I wanted to talk.

"Nah.  I think I'll get to bed, too," I said casually, angling my head toward Brown's partially open bedroom door.

# Chapter Fourteen

Things were back to normal the following morning as we boarded the chopper.  The flight was uneventful and I spent the next couple of days readjusting to my apartment until White called me down to his.

As soon as I stepped in he instructed me to take a seat on his couch. He went to the war room and came back with another sealed manila envelope.

"I haven't checked this out, but it's another job outside of the company."

I opened the envelope and pulled out the material. This time White was curious about the contents and waited for me to hand him the paperwork.

"This job comes from an entirely different source than before," he explained his curiosity.

"Who?"

"The Russian government."

I was shocked. "Why would I work for the Russians?"

"You don't have to accept the job. Read through it and then hand it over."

I turned the pages over and was met with a picture of Dimitri Glaskov and a picture of the new and improved Dimitri as Mr. Prutko. I handed the photos to White and started to read the next page.

| | |
|---|---|
| *Subject:* | *Dimitri Glaskov; AKA Anatoli Prutko* |
| *Mission:* | *Target Elimination* |
| *Location:* | *Unknown* |

The rest of the page was filled with more information about Dimitri that was relevant to his appearance and possible locations. For example, The Rave and Gigi's were listed as assets and other businesses believed to belong to him. Even suspected places of residence.

I handed this to White when I finished reading and was greeted with satellite photos of all the locations listed. I set these aside and found a sheet that listed a bank and an account number with the words: *Half of the account balance is available if the mission is accepted, the other half will be released after mission completion.*

The next bundle of paper work read like a book report on Dimitri Glaskov. I learned his place of birth, parents' names and current locations, which happened to be in a cemetery somewhere in St. Petersburg. The information seemed to go on and on, listing everything personal I could ever want to know about Dimitri Glaskov, AKA Anatoli Prutko.

I sat on White's couch, trying to take it all in. The Russian government was hiring me to take out Dimitri Glaskov. How did they know how to find me? What made them think I would do a job like this? How did they even know he was still alive? The last time I checked, no one knew he was still alive except White and Associates, Colin and my father.

"So?" White interrupted my thoughts.

"So, what? I don't know why I would get asked to do a job like this."

"You've already done a job like this," he reminded me.

"Yeah, but that was for my father."

"I didn't say it was," White said.

"It wasn't for my father?" I was even more shocked.

"Well, yeah, it was, but it could have been from anywhere. We weren't supposed to know who it came from and we aren't supposed to know where this job came from either. I found a way around that."

"But why me? How did anyone know that they could contact *me*?"

"They don't know who you are. They only know where to submit the requests," he explained.

"So, if I take this job, no one will know I did it?"

"Just me."

I thought about it and considered calling my father.

White read my mind and said, "You can't ask advice on this. This is between you and I. You run the risk of exposure if you talk to anyone else about this."

I gathered the paperwork and headed into C.I.C. White followed me without a word. I went directly to a computer and signed onto the government database with my special password.

Dimitri's information had been updated and I discovered something new. They'd lost track of him. I noticed the date of his last known position and it was two days after my hit on Grigori.

I started to put it together. I'd done the Grigori job, Dimitri had found the bug and then he fell off the map. I assumed the death of his son had led to the finding of the bug which in turn led to Dimitri going back into hiding.

What made anyone think he could be found if he had successfully hidden himself for five years prior to his recent reappearance?

White and I discussed all the ramifications of me taking the job and of me not taking the job. Provided I completed the mission and didn't get caught, it was in everyone's best interest to take out Dimitri before he could re-establish himself too firmly. I immediately started my search. White gave me permission to use my teams how I saw fit, but only to locate Dimitri, and he promised to help in any way he could.

I spent the entire day and night researching the locations and known associates that had been given to me. Most of them weren't worth looking into. The Rave and Gigi's were two of the least likely places he'd be at right now. They were his most recent known locations and if he had any brains he wouldn't show his face in either place ever again. Also, all known associates should already be under heavy surveillance.

Still, I looked into them and found some interesting information. Both clubs were for sale. I filed this away for future research and started sending men out to other different locations to do some surveillance. Their instructions were to report to either White or myself and no one else.

I gave each team a location and instructions to report all activity as well as taking pictures of all people in the vicinity. All the information and pictures were to be sent to us immediately.

When the reports started coming in White and I spent hours going over the intelligence sent from each team and weren't rewarded with any leads. This became a daily task.

In between the reports and pictures sent by my teams I spent some time researching Dimitri's history. This wasn't as hard as I expected because all the information I could want was just waiting for me in the paperwork I'd received. I double checked most of it on the government database and found they had most but not all of his personal background. I took the time to enter what they didn't have into the database, hoping this might help them to find Dimitri. I didn't see any problem with getting unwitting outside help.

The first time I'd logged onto the database with my new password I hadn't covered my tracks but the nature of my searches inspired a new paranoia and I made sure my location could not be tracked.

White and I worked closely together for two weeks with no positive results. I brought up my previous thought about not knowing how we'd find Dimitri when the entire government couldn't find him.

"We're better than them. Plus we aren't under the same restrictions."

I rolled my eyes and tried to think of new ideas. We'd almost exhausted all of the information given to us by the Russians and that I found on my own.

"About all we have left are Gigi's and The Rave." I sighed.

"He wouldn't go back there," White shook his head.

"I know, but they are for sale. If they sold, the money would more than likely find its way back to Dimitri."

"Yeah," he was thoughtful. "Do you want to invest in property?"

"Not really. It's a long shot and I don't think I should go back to Gigi's for anything."

"I suppose you're right," the two of us sat quietly. Before long White said, "We could let the government take the risk. They have more money to play with and I'm sure they'd like to find Dimitri too."

"But how do we get them to do the work for us? I've already tried by adding all the info I got from the Russian's into their database."

"I could give the Admiral a call to ask him about Dimitri? Hey..." his face lit up. "What about Sal? We could ask the Admiral if we could interrogate him."

"Do you think Sal would know anything? And if he did, don't you think my father would already have gotten it out of him?"

"Search him on the database," he pointed to the computer beside me.

White's order made me think of something else. I hadn't researched any of Dimitri's contacts that were locked up or being held in secret detainment facilities. What if there were contacts out there that weren't listed in the paperwork I'd gotten from the Russians or from the database?

I swiveled in my chair and started my search. I knew Sal was a long shot but searched him first to placate White. My prediction that Sal wouldn't know anything important was proven true so I continued to cross reference the name Dimitri Glaskov with all names in the database. I knew this would take some time so I rose to get coffee.

"What are you doing now?" White followed me to his kitchen.

I explained the idea he'd inspired and he gave me an approving nod.

We sat quietly in his kitchen while we waited for the computers to find anything we might be able to use. The quiet didn't last long before there was a knock at White's door.

He opened it to Black.

"The two of you have been spending a lot of time together lately," he pressed. If he only knew, I thought.

"Yeah, we've been working on something for the Admiral," White explained it away.

"Ah," Black sounded disappointed. "You look tired," he told me.

"I am."

"Must be pretty important?" He was fishing for information that I couldn't give him.

"Yes, it is," White cut in, letting Black know the conversation was over. I hated doing this. I didn't like keeping secrets and had never been good at lying, especially to people I cared for.

"Excuse me," I went back into C.I.C. to check the computer. I heard Black and White talking in the kitchen.

"Don't forget our conversation," Black sounded ominous.

"Don't worry and believe me, I wouldn't expect any less from you. We really are working on something. Nothing has happened and if it does, she'll be in good hands."

"I know your track record. She's good for the company and if you screw that up..."

"I know. I've given this a lot of thought and my intentions are honorable. But, like I said, we are working on something right now. Those feelings haven't even surfaced." I heard footsteps coming toward C.I.C.

"Alex," I turned at the sound of Black's voice.

"Yes?" I couldn't hide my feelings of guilt for the outside job and my feelings for White.

"I apologize for being insensitive at the cabin." He was having a hard time looking at me. His gaze wandered from my face to the floor and back to my face.

I walked past him and shut the door so White wouldn't over hear our conversation. I knew this was going to be hard for me but even worse for Black.

"Absolutely no hard feelings," I smiled.

"Good. If things get too intense, let me know." He'd become more confident after I'd shut the door. I'd never seen Black this way.

"I think we all work well together and am afraid to make any changes that could jeopardize that, but..." I struggled for words to explain.

"If you take that step, make sure it works. And if it doesn't work, you make sure *that* works. Understand?"

"Yes." I understood and agreed with him.

"Good." He let the door to C.I.C. hang open when he left.

White rejoined me. "What was that about?" He didn't realize I'd overheard their conversation.

"The same thing he talked to you about," I blushed.

"Alex, I'm not as bad as he says," White tried to explain.

"He didn't say anything about you. He's looking out for the company." We stood for a few seconds, contemplating each other, before I turned back to the computer.

It had compiled some names from its search and I pressed print. The printer near White started to spit out pages and when it was done he brought them over to me.

There were only three pages but they were full of names. I estimated we had close to one hundred to search through. I was skimming through them when White asked me for a page so he could help me. I handed over the first page and moved my eyes quickly over the second page and laid it on the table for him when he was ready.

I took more time with the third page, knowing he'd be busy with the first two. I reached the R's and recognized a name. James Ruben. My father used to have a close acquaintance with that name. I'd not seen him or heard my father speak of him for years. Then again, I'd been out of the house and most day-to-day conversations since I went to college.

Curiosity got the better of me and I turned back to the database and looked him up. My stomach plummeted to the floor when his picture loaded. It *was* the man I used to know. He and my father worked together and I knew my father held him in close confidence. I poured over the information in the database and hoped he'd been investigating Dimitri and that was why his name was brought up. However, as I read, I knew this wouldn't be the case because I'd searched only names listed as incarcerated or detained.

James Ruben was listed as a threat to national security and a flight risk. He'd been selling secrets to several factions, the Russian Mafia being only one outlet for his treason. He'd never been brought to trial because of lack of evidence but instead was *detained* until a case could be brought against him. The authorizing signature was Robert S. Stanton.

"What have you got?" White brought me back to the present.

"I know him," I sounded as ill as I felt.

White leaned over me to see the screen. I explained what I knew and what I'd just read.

I continued to read as White hung over my shoulder. There was no further information of any importance other than what I'd already found out.

"Do you think this could be useful?" White sounded dubious.

"I don't know," I was still shocked.

"They've had him in custody for five years so I don't think he'd be able to help us find Dimitri. Chances are he still thinks he's dead."

"No, he was taken into custody before Dimitri faked his death," I pointed out.

"I really don't think we'd get in to see him or any other detainees. The government doesn't even admit to holding most of these people." White was still doubtful.

"I'm sure your right. I'm just surprised that my father would do this to his friend."

"Look at the list of offenses. He wasn't your father's friend."

"I suppose not." I scrolled the screen down to finish my reading, knowing it would be fruitless. But, when I reached the bottom of the report there was one notation. Ruben had been released ten hours ago. The authorizing signature was *Lt. Commander Colin DeLange.*

White had regained his seat and was reading the pages I'd printed when I interrupted him with this news.

"Really? Now, that is interesting. Still, not much we can do on that angle without risking detection. I'm sure he's under heavy surveillance."

James Ruben was a man I knew from the beginning of time. He'd been to our home on several occasions and I never knew what he really was. I couldn't imagine how my father felt once he figured out Ruben's betrayals. I knew White was right; there wasn't anything we could do here so I went back to researching the other names.

After hours of reading and cross referencing we only found two possible leads. We knew we wouldn't be able to speak to any of Dimitri's past contacts but we could send some men to check out their friends and family on the outside.

I looked at the time before calling out a team and it was after two in the morning.

"White, I'm going home but I'll be back first thing in the morning," I yawned.

He checked the time and nodded as he rose to walk me out.

"I appreciate all your help with this," I said as I stepped out the door.

"How about dinner, just the two…" he was stopped short by his phone ringing. "Wait here, this could be important."

I stepped back into his apartment and shut the door.

"Yes," White answered the phone.

"Yes, sir." Must be my father, I thought. I'd never heard White address anyone else as sir. White abruptly hung up the phone and started putting on his shoes.

"Well?"

"That was the Admiral.  You and I are supposed to meet him at the office in a few minutes."

"Did he say what for?"

"Nope."  He'd finished putting on his shoes and was making his way to the door.

# Chapter Fifteen

My father and Colin walked through the door of the office within minutes after our arrival.

Colin looked absolutely miserable and I felt a pang of sympathy for him. I didn't know what was going on but knew it must be important for them to show up at this hour and for Colin to look so dejected. I hope no one had been killed.

"White. Grey," my father greeted us in a sober voice. "I need your services. Mr. DeLange," the omission of his rank wasn't lost on any of us, "has made a grievous error and I need your help to rectify it."

"Of course, Admiral," White answered.

Colin was trying to hold his head up but I watched as he dropped his gaze to the floor more than once.

"Mr. DeLange has released a potentially dangerous criminal into the population, thinking he could keep tabs on him. However, the man is exceptionally talented and within hours of release has evaded our supervision." He paused for several seconds. "I have no paperwork to give you but the man's name is James Ruben. We worked closely for many years before I found out he was a traitor. He was selling information to several different groups. One of which was the Russian Mafia." None of this was news to White and me but we couldn't say anything.

"I remember him," I put in.

"I supposed you would. Dimitri has also gone missing, however, we've recently acquired his location. Mr. DeLange thought, because of Ruben's and Dimitri's past, Ruben could possibly lead us to Dimitri and we'd have enough evidence to convict the both of them. However, there are details about Ruben known only to me. The man is a threat to more than just the country and should never have been released." He looked meaningfully at me.

"What are these details?" I asked.

"She is going to retire," he seemed to be speaking to himself. "I have given this a lot of thought and think it prudent for Commander DeLange to know certain facts that only we are privy to. He *is* going to take my place in the company as well as the government and I feel I can trust him with all of my information."

I knew what this meant. He was going to tell Colin who Penumbra was. I had mixed emotions on this subject but he'd said she was going to retire.

"Are you sure?" This was my mother, after all. I knew Colin could be trusted with the info but I still believed the less people who knew, the better.

"Yes, Alex. I don't see any other way around it if we are to protect her."

"Who?" Colin's attitude had entirely changed. He was full of curiosity now.

The silence was thick until White said, "Penumbra."

The air in the room was heavy before this utterance but now it could have smothered us all had Colin not repeated the name, "Penumbra?  She's a *she?*  You know who Penumbra is?" His last question was directed at me.

"Yes.  So do you," Colin gave me a strange look when I said this.  "She's my mother."

The realization on his face was as dramatic as if he'd practiced gaining this knowledge for years.

"Ruben knows who Penumbra is and that is the reason I had him detained.  All of the allegations are true," my father added to make sure we knew he wasn't holding Ruben under false pretenses.  "I would have had him killed years ago if I thought I could get away with it. That kind of information cannot be ignored.  He is a very well known man throughout the entire world on both sides of the game.  I am the only person who's known where he was these past few years.  I should have taken the risk years ago to protect Penumbra but because of his connections and our previous friendship I put him under lock and key. He's not had contact with anyone but me for more than five years and his mental health has declined.  He's very unpredictable and I don't know where he'd go.  It is possible he may contact Dimitri so I'd like you to set up surveillance around him.  We need to keep an eye on him anyway."  I looked at White with relief.  Finally we were going to be able to finish the job I'd taken on.

"I need White and Associates to locate Ruben but I'm asking for an outside job as well," Colin's ears perked up again when he heard the Admiral mention an outside job.

"Ruben must be eliminated once he's found," the Admiral looked directly at me.

"Of course," I didn't hesitate.  I knew this was the only course of action if my mother was to be saved.

I watched Colin's face.  He was the only person in this room that didn't fully appreciate my role outside the company.  Again, I wasn't disappointed.  The look of shock on his face actually made me smile.  Now he knew exactly how much I could take care of myself.

"You look ill, Commander DeLange," White was also openly grinning.

"I," he paused to compose himself.  "I didn't realize you would involve her in situations like this," he accused White.

"He didn't," my father stopped the potential argument.  "I did. She's been in training for this since she was born."  Now it was my turn for a wake-up call.  Everything was clear to me now.  It hit me all at once and I knew my true role wasn't that of Alexis Stanton, daughter of

Mr. and Mrs. Stanton. It wasn't Alex Stanton, data processor. It wasn't even Ms. Grey. I stood from my seat, ready to object to my revelation.

"Not now, Alex," the Admiral rose from his seat. "Soon enough. Here," he reached inside his jacket and pulled out another sealed envelope. I knew what was inside and didn't want to touch it. Tears welled up into my eyes.

"But," I was breathing heavily.

"Decide, right now. You know you can do it." He held the envelope out to me.

I looked at White who sat with an unreadable expression. The tears had welled higher into my eyes and a single drop flowed down my cheek as I took the envelope. Internally I was saying goodbye to Alexis Stanton and Ms. Grey. Nothing would ever be the same again.

Colin had come into this meeting not knowing what we knew and was leaving without full comprehension. I assumed the Admiral would tell him, eventually. I'd let him pick the time.

As soon as Colin and the Admiral had left the office I turned on White.

"You knew! This whole time you knew!"

"Well, yes, but in my defense, I didn't know from the moment of your birth."

"Did you know when I came looking for the job?" I wanted to know if he and my father had set me up to become a partner in White and Associates.

"No. I've only known for a few months. But, your father was the one who suggested we take on a female partner. The ad you answered had been running in the paper for almost a year before you found it. You wouldn't believe the people I had to turn down. Though none of them were you, anyway."

My emotions were tangled and confused. "Would I have gotten the partnership if my last name hadn't been Stanton?"

"Yes," White's answer was simple and quick.

"Even if I wasn't the one my father had *set up*?" I spat the last two words out as if they tasted vile.

"Even if you weren't the one. We'd just have two female partners." He looked at me closely. "Alex, you are more than qualified for any job that comes your way. Of course you still have things to learn; but we all do. Don't let your father's plan make you think you don't have what it takes. You do."

I considered his words and decided they would do for now. "We better get to work moving the teams around,"

"My thoughts, exactly." He came over to me and pulled me into an embrace. After what seemed like an eternity our lips parted.

"Finally," he sighed.   Finally, I thought but couldn't say anything. Taking me by the hand he led me to the elevator.

---

Black showed up early that morning at White's apartment. White put him to work helping us rearrange the teams we hadn't gotten to yet. Now that we really had a job from the Admiral we could let the rest of the partners in on some of the details.

A lot of the people and places under surveillance didn't change. Most of Rubens contacts were also associates of Dimitri. Not a lot of rearranging needed to be done so all we needed to do was wait.

I considered taking out Dimitri immediately but decided against it just in case Ruben did try to contact him. We still had the same problems as before but with a different person. We were still looking for a man whose identity couldn't be revealed to anyone.

My mother showed up, accompanied by Colin. I took them to my apartment and helped her get settled in. She'd be staying with me until Ruben was found. My mother was obviously put out and the look of awe on Colin's face every time he looked at her was priceless.

"Your father thinks I need to be here," she began.

"You do, Mom. Let us do our job and be nice to Colin."

"He didn't even tell me about Ruben. Can you believe that? I could have fixed this years ago." She was furious.

"I know, but now I'll do it."

"I know you will, honey," her tone changed as she rubbed her hand down my hair. "I've always known."

"I know," now it was my turn to have an angry tone. "Colin, I know my father told you to stay, but I'm telling you to leave. If you stay, it'll raise more questions than if my mother comes for a visit. We need to keep this between us and it doesn't help if we raise eyebrows."

He started to object but one look at my mother was enough to shut him up and he left without a word. My mother and I giggled as soon as the door shut behind him.

"Ah, the power of a name," she laughed.

"Ah, the danger of a name," I played on her words.  I made sure she was comfortable and left her alone to go back to C.I.C.

---

White was alone when I returned.

"We should get you into position," he said.

"But how are we going to explain my absence to the partners?"

"I've got that worked out. I have another prospect whose reports will be credited to you. Don't forget, I'm the only one who see's the reports. No one else knows who we are looking for or that we'll be watching Dimitri. The Admiral has men attached to him right now but once you are in place he'll call them off."

"Won't the guys get suspicious if you send me out alone? And what about the hit? Don't you think they'll put things together afterwards?" I didn't know how to go about all this secrecy.

"No. It's not unusual that you'd go out to help your team with something like this. It won't mean you took out Dimitri just because you happened to be in the vicinity when it happens. Don't forget, the men don't know you've actually completed any missions of this type. You'll have the go ahead as soon as we locate Ruben and maybe before, if it's possible Dimitri is going to relocate."

It was suspected he'd left the country so most of their manpower had been focused in that direction until someone read the new information I had entered into the database. Dimitri had never left the city, which was a risk, but one that had paid off until Colin's men located some old friends of his family.

I loaded up my gear and met White at the office to retrieve my rifle.

"I've rented you a car under a false name. It's in the parking garage," he tossed me the keys. "I also managed to talk the Admiral into allowing us access to the house across the street that his men have been using. He doesn't know it's you who will be taking over surveillance so do not enter the premises until you are sure it's unoccupied. It's fully stocked so you won't have to leave for anything. If you do need something, contact me. The Admiral's men should be packing up as we speak so the house should be empty when you get there."

I left the office building in the rented car and found myself at the destination in less than half an hour. Parking the car two blocks away, I made my way to the house from behind and did a thorough perimeter check as well as looking through every window I could. It seemed uninhabited so I gained entrance through the back door. After a quick check I was sure the men had packed up and weren't going to come back.

The house was in a quiet neighborhood. I wasn't looking forward to breaking the peace in an area like this, but I might have to. White had set me up with a night vision binoculars and a long distance listening device. I was glad he hadn't sent much more in case I had to make a quick exit.

I sent hourly reports to White through my phone for a full day. I was getting anxious. I'd seen Dimitri several times, though he never left the house. There were two other men who, upon orders, left the house to get food. Leaving me the perfect opportunity to complete my mission. However, I was under strict orders not to do so, yet.

Through White, I learned that the house had belonged to Russian immigrants who'd been friends of Dimitri's parents. Neither of them were still alive but the house was still in their names so Dimitri thought he could stay there undetected. How long he'd be satisfied with this arrangement was still up in the air. However, he'd made mention to his men, after they returned, about making preparations to move on.

I kept a close eye on things after Dimitri mentioned he didn't know how much longer he'd stay. The men didn't seem to be making any solid preparations. No phone calls were made for any transportation but that didn't mean they hadn't made the arrangements during their trip away from the house. Dimitri didn't bring up leaving again after the one seemingly off-hand remark.

I was having a tough time staying awake after dark. I'd already been up for several days without a break. If I were outside I might be able to stay alert, I thought to myself. But I knew being outside in a situation like this would just complicate my ability to remain invisible. I didn't even dare open the windows for fear of someone noticing a change in the house's appearance. I got up and started pacing the floor while Dimitri and his men were watching television. I kept the earphones on while I paced so my range was limited.

Fifteen minutes before I was scheduled to report to White I received a call. White said pictures of Ruben were forwarded to him from a location inside the city.

"This would be much easier if we could tell the men exactly who to look for and have them tail him. Those pictures are useless."

"Not entirely. Now we know he's in the area."

"But why? Does he know Dimitri is in town? If he does, how does he know? I need to take care of Dimitri and then we can start to actively search for Ruben. I could be out of here in less than five minutes and we could go to Ruben's last known location. He can only be so far away."

"I'm already on my way there. You need to sit tight."

"I don't see why," I complained. I really didn't think keeping Dimitri alive was going to help matters.

After Ruben had been sighted I didn't have any more problems staying awake and was diligent with my surveillance. I thought about taking Dimitri out over and over. Every possible scene played through my head. My biggest worry were the two extra men in the house. I knew I could easily take Dimitri. He had a tendency to stand near the kitchen window and stare out. My current view through my scope was exactly that, Dimitri at the kitchen window. The other men, however, rarely neared the windows and I wondered why they'd allow the man under their protection to stand there.

Shortly after I questioned his bodyguard's abilities I was rewarded with why they didn't say much.

"You know you shouldn't stand in the window, boss." I heard one of the men tell him.

"I only have you here to play fetch!" His Russian accent was almost overwhelming when he was angry. "In fact, go get me," he took a moment to think, "I feel like some vanilla ice cream. Fetch, dogs!"

The men left without a word but once outside they complained about Dimitri's lack of respect for them. I listened to them complain until they sped off.

Again, another missed chance, I thought as I watched Dimitri move through the house. His actions were deliberate, making me wonder what he was up to. I didn't have to wait long to realize his intentions. The garage door opened and he started to back a car down the driveway. He was going to leave while his men were gone.

I had to take the shot. Thoughts of my mother and Ruben wandering around with his knowledge flashed through my mind but I didn't hesitate long. I felt the kick of my weapon and the sound echoed through the house, making my ears ring.

My scope lingered just long enough to be sure the bullet had found its place and realize the car was still moving backward. It was coming quickly down the driveway and I knew if it didn't lose some momentum it would crash right through my front door.

I gathered my equipment and was at the back of the house in seconds. As I opened the door to exit I felt the whole house shake and heard a muffled crash. Though I knew the sound would have been loud, the ringing in my ears dampened it somewhat. The next thing I knew, I was at Dimitri's side in the living room. The car had deviated just enough to miss the front door and crash through the front bay window I'd recently shot out. I pulled a sealed manila envelope from inside my jacket. It was inside a plastic baggie to protect it from collecting evidence. It was the same as the one Team Grey had placed near the bodies I'd left in Alaska. The small business card inside carried no weight compared to the envelope itself. I shook it out of the baggie and watched it flutter into Dimitri's lap and raced out the back door and down the street to my waiting car.

Shaking, I checked my speedometer and knew I better slow it down. I hadn't taken the time to stow my equipment in the trunk and if I got pulled over I'd have a lot of explaining to do. Who drove around with a .50 cal sniper rifle in the back seat?

Regularly checking my speed I decided I better tell White I'd completed the mission, for better or for worse. I dialed his number and waited for him to answer. By the third ring he still hadn't answered and terrible things began to flash through my mind. I immediately thought of Evans and wondered if Ruben was holding White hostage. The phone rang for the fourth time and he picked up.

"I was just trying to call you," he said. "You need to get out of the house. The Admiral has sent men back to watch Dimitri while we take care of Ruben."

"He's not going anywhere," I replied coldly.

"Good. You'll have to tell me about it later," White then went on to explain the pictures of Ruben had been taken near my parents' house. He was still there, probably hoping to confront the Admiral. I needed to meet White there so we could take care of Ruben.

I turned the vehicle toward my new destination but was still careful to obey traffic laws. My foot wanted to push to the floor but I held it in check all the way there.

I spotted White's car immediately and pulled up behind him. I stepped out of the vehicle and quickly ducked inside next to White.

"So, what's the plan?" I looked around for Ruben.

"He's inside," White indicated the house with a nod of his head. "We'll have to get him out of there," White's plan was interrupted by the sight of my puke green mustang pulling up the driveway.

"That was my mother," I breathed. I sat for two more seconds before I jumped from White's vehicle and ran up the driveway. I faintly heard White running behind me. My hearing had fully recovered from the earlier gunshot but now my heartbeat was pounding in my ears.

I reached the front door and noticed it had been left open. White circled around the back as I confidently crossed the threshold. My mother was standing in the middle of the room and Ruben had a gun trained on her.

"Ruben," she was saying. "You know this isn't true. Why would Robert have you detained for five years?"

Ruben was disheveled and wild looking.

"Because I know who you are." He noticed me standing there and moved the gun toward me. "Get over here," he ordered me to stand near my mother.

"Mr. Ruben," I played her game. "What's going on?"

"Your mother is Penumbra and I'm going to stop her."

"What are you talking about? She's not Penumbra," I countered as I moved into position.

Ruben reached inside his pocket and pulled out a phone. He tossed it at me. "Call your Dad and tell him to get home!" He was becoming even more agitated.

I did as I was told and called the Admiral. He said he was on his way and I relayed the message to Ruben.

"Put the phone on the floor and kick it back to me," Ruben ordered again. Again I did as I was told.

"Alexis, I'm sorry about this but I'm going to have to kill you and your mother now," he took aim at my mother.

"No," I stepped in front of her. This allowed White enough time to cross the distance to Ruben.

The years in jail hadn't hurt Ruben's reflexes and he turned and fired. White dropped to the floor and I heard myself scream. All sense left me and I started to advance on Ruben.

"Explain to me why you're here, Ruben," my slow advance made him falter.

"Your father put me in a detainment camp for five years because I know what your mother is! You all will die for that!"

"You think my mother is Penumbra?" I was incredulous.

"I know she is."

"Then you don't know the truth. She is not Penumbra," I paused for dramatic effect then added, "I am."

I'd closed the distance between us and now he was within reach. I dove for his legs just as he fired at me. He missed but I didn't. He fell to the ground and the gun was knocked from his hand. It skittered across the hardwood floor and my mother ran for it.

She had the gun trained on the both of us before we stood from our tumble.

"You wanted the truth, Ruben. Now you have it. Meet Penumbra," my mother said just as I landed a punch across his jaw. He fell to the floor once again.

Cowering on the floor he whimpered, "But you were a child." He was obviously confused.

"I was. You've messed with the wrong family." I let him regain his feet. My mother tossed me the gun and I shot him at point blank range. Hot blood splattered my face and the smell almost made me gag.

I turned to White, lying on the floor. He was taking short breaths.

"You *are* Penumbra," his face held the same awe Colin wore when he looked at my mother.

"Shhh," I said as I moved around to cradle his head. I didn't know tears were streaming down my face until one dropped onto White's forehead. I took a deep breath and told my mother to make sure the Admiral was bringing medical help.

"The Admiral?" She questioned me as she dug in Ruben's pocket for the phone. This made me realize I'd been calling him the Admiral since I found out what he'd been training me for my whole life.

"You shouldn't be so hard on your father," she said as she dialed. "I had to threaten divorce to get him to agree to your training."

For some reason, my mother planning my entire life wasn't as offensive as if it had been my father.

My father, Colin and all of my partners showed up in the chopper minutes later. Blue immediately came to White's side.

"Are you okay, buddy?" he asked White.

"Oh, just great," White's voice was weak.

"Well, you've lost some blood. We've got to get you to the hospital." The rest of the partners had accumulated around us. Black reached down and pulled White up by his arms. Red came around to his feet and lifted him into the air.

I remained on the floor, unable to move, until Blue said, "Grey, we've got to hurry." This brought me out of my stupor and I jumped up and followed them to the chopper.

After White's surgery my partners and I sat near his side. Eventually they each took their leave but I remained. It was because of me White had been shot. I shouldn't have run into the house. I should have grabbed my rifle and taken Ruben from a distance.

Early the next morning Colin woke me up gently.

"He's still asleep?"

"Yes. But the doctors say he should wake up soon."

"Alex, I just want to apologize," Colin said sincerely.

"What for?"

"What for? For letting that lunatic out. For not giving you enough credit." This last sentence was barely audible.

"Colin," I began, but he cut me off.

"No. I truly am sorry."

"Colin," I started again. "It wasn't your fault you let Ruben go. My father should have informed you of everything before he gave you the power. You couldn't have known. As for not giving me enough credit..." I smirked at him.

"Speaking of," his look became one of pride.   "Dimitri Glaskov was found dead last night, with a bullet right between the eyes. Can you guess who's calling card was in his lap?"

"I bet I could," I answered.

"Oh, the Admiral told me to tell you that Ruben can't be attributed to Penumbra.  Too many witnesses."

White stirred in his hospital bed.  I turned toward him and took his hand.

"Alex?" he asked before he opened his eyes.

"I'm here."

"Good," he fell back to sleep.

Colin stayed an hour longer then left me alone with White again.

White recovered after several weeks in the hospital and another with me at his beck and call in his apartment.  Finally, the feelings of guilt dissipated and I told him to get his own coffee.

"But you do it so well," he chided.

"Maybe so, but I'm sick of it," I watched him climb from the couch.  He grunted and groaned as he tried to stand and I grinned, knowing most of it was for show.  When he reached the coffee pot in the kitchen I yelled, "Grab me a cup while you're up."

CPSIA information can be obtained at www.ICGtesting.com
Printed in the USA
LVOW07s1217260913

354117LV00045B/1036/P